. . . Sonya quickened her pace — moving her face slowly down towards the very center of the fine fragrance that lured her.

. . . Sonya's tongue began to slowly travel into the forest, parting the soft hair, making a pathway; her lovemaking was so very new — yet so very familiar

. . . Sonya, o please, Sonya." Margeaux was lost in sensation.

"That's right, sweet one, that's right, let me hear you moan," Sonya murmured, lifting her face from the luscious forest, watching Margeaux purring, panting, slightly arching. . .

pleasures

by Robbi Sommers

pleasures

by Robbi Sommers

The Naiad Press, Inc.
1989

Printed in the United States of America
First Edition

Edited by Christi Cassidy
Cover design by Pat Tong and Bonnie Liss
    (Phoenix Graphics)
Typeset by Sandi Stancil

Library of Congress Cataloging-in-Publication Data

Sommers, Robbi, 1950—
    Pleasures / by Robbi Sommers.
        p.   cm.
    Contents: Lydia — Elyse — Julia — Ginger —
Miss Lavender — Lilith — Roberta — Morrigan — Sayre —
Victoria — Margeaux — Jesse.
    ISBN 0-941483-49-5 : $8.95
    1. Lesbians—Fiction. 2. Erotic stories, American.   I. Title.
PS3569.065335P5   1989
813.54—dc20   89-33963
                                                          CIP

The goddess, Inanna, took my hand
And led me down, deep into my Self.
To this journey, I dedicate my book.

Grateful acknowledgment to the women
who helped me to face myself:

Donna, TK, and Sara.

About the Author

Robbi Sommers was born in Cincinnati, Ohio in 1950. She now lives in Sonoma County, California, where she spends her days working as a Dental Hygienist and her evenings . . . creating fantasies.

Contents

LYDIA

It was six months since Carolyn had dated anyone.
Six months since she had decided not to be sexual. It
just hadn't worked. Every time she felt an attraction
for any of the women she met, anytime she ended up
in bed with one of them, no matter what happened,
she was not able to have an orgasm. Frustrated and
embarrassed, Carolyn had decided to back off from
the dating scene and spend some time alone. Until
yesterday.

Yesterday at lunch, Maxine had been rambling on
about her friend Louisa who had seen this

1

gynecologist in Berkeley and how impressed she had been. How this doctor had made Louisa so comfortable — relaxed. Like the doctor really cared. Such a rare thing these days and . . .

For some reason Carolyn became more than interested. Perhaps this was where she could turn with her problem — her inability to climax — maybe she could feel safe enough with this doctor to finally talk about her secret.

And here she was, the next day, in traffic, for over an hour, in the heat, on her way to Berkeley to see Dr. Baronson. If she could get up the nerve, maybe she could get some help with her situation. Perhaps she was built wrong? Perhaps she needed to relax more? Perhaps she needed to learn some new techniques.

When she had called, the receptionist said they were booked, booked for three weeks in advance. Was this an emergency? What, in fact, was the problem?

And Carolyn had meekly, barely audibly muttered to the receptionist her problem. And no, of course it wasn't an emergency, but it was her day off tomorrow, and she was quite concerned about her problem, and — "Oh yes, of course. Just a minute please," the receptionist had said with such a tone of compassion that Carolyn felt okay about having told her of her dilemma.

And that was it. The receptionist was able to squeeze her in. The doctor would come back from lunch early tomorrow just to see Carolyn.

Now ten minutes away. Now five minutes away. Onto Shattuck, down, turn left, three blocks, turn right. The first Victorian house on the left.

Carolyn parked the car and felt overcome with

2

nervousness. What in heaven's name had she done? Blurted out her problem to a complete stranger! Now she was going to face this doctor and most probably be more embarrassed than she'd ever been in her life. Almost ready to jump back into her car and get out of there, Carolyn tried to reevaluate the situation carefully.

I don't want to fake orgasms anymore, she thought. I want to be like the women I have sex with. I want to be able to relax, feel good, get that incredible pleasure everyone except me seems to experience. This doctor is supposed to be so caring and understanding. She already has agreed to shorten her lunch hour just to see me. She'll probably be very kind and reassuring — and more than that, she'll be able to give me some help with my problem.

Through the large stained glass doors of the old Victorian house, the reception room was bright and very cheerful. Leafy green plants filled the corners. Stained glass windows, antique furniture. It was beautiful and welcoming.

Carolyn picked up a magazine and sat in a plush, comfortable velvet chair. Within minutes a door opened and a pleasant blonde-haired woman poked her head out.

"Carolyn?" she asked sweetly.

"Yes," Carolyn responded, placing the magazine back on the table.

"Hi, I'm Dr. Baronson," she said, opening the door wider. "Unfortunately, my nurse and receptionist are still at lunch, so I'm going to have to play their roles, too." She continued with a pleasing laugh, "Please come this way."

Carolyn was surprised. She had expected someone

3

older, more mature — even matronly. And instead, she found herself following a very attractive woman who appeared to be in her early thirties.

Dr. Baronson was wearing a dark blue, tight skirt with a slit that exposed a hint of her full calf. A cream-colored silk blouse. A white lab coat. Dark blue high heels. Dark hose. Her platinum blonde hair was pulled back severely into a tight French twist. Round tortoise-shell glasses made her look slightly older. More professional than her young face seemed to suggest.

Carolyn followed Dr. Baronson into a small room and sat in a corner chair as directed.

"Now," Dr. Baronson said softly. "Lydia, my receptionist, mentioned that you were having some problems that were troubling you quite a bit. Would you like to share them with me?"

There was something about her voice, her face, her tone, that created an intense feeling of trust and safety. Maxine's friend Louisa was right. Carolyn had never felt so at ease with anyone.

As Carolyn began to explain her sexual difficulty, Dr. Baronson did not say much, nodding occasionally, making notes on a small pad. Yet Carolyn could sense her compassion.

"And so, that's why I'm here," Carolyn concluded shyly. "Is there anything I can do?"

"Well, first of all," Dr. Baronson replied confidently, pushing her round glasses up higher onto the bridge of her nose, "I think we should find out if your problem is physical or emotional. I'll need to give you a complete exam. If everything is in working order, we can rule out the physical and go on to the next step. How does that sound?"

"Well, I guess that would be okay," Carolyn said, shifting slightly in the chair.

"Good!" Dr. Baronson stood up. "Please undress completely, put on this gown and then get up on the table. I'll be back in a few minutes."

As Carolyn removed her clothes and put on the light green gown, she felt a small wave of happiness pass through her. I am finally doing something about this problem, she thought excitedly. Her thinking was interrupted by Dr. Baronson's quick knock on the door.

Carolyn lay back on the table, put her feet in the stirrups and slid down towards the end of the examination table.

"Good," said Dr. Baronson. "I've never liked these tables," she continued in the same gentle tone, "because my patients feel so uncomfortable, or exposed, if you will. But I haven't found anything that worked as well. So please bear with me and I apologize for any discomfort."

"Oh, that's okay," Carolyn replied, aware of her own slight uneasiness. Closing her eyes she let her legs fall to each side. The doctor's kindness and understanding were making the experience almost bearable.

"Now," Dr. Baronson said as she seated herself at the end of the table, simultaneously adjusting a small light between Carolyn's legs. "I'm going to tell you what I am doing as I am doing it. If you have any questions or comments, please feel free to interrupt me. Okay?"

"Yes, that's fine," answered Carolyn.

"Okay then. First, I'm going to spread your lips apart. That's right, just relax. I'm going to spread

5

you apart so I can get a good look at your clitoral shaft. Yes. Can you feel this? I don't have you stretched too far do I?"

"No," Carolyn said quietly, a little embarrassed.

"Fine." Dr. Baronson continued, "Let's see. What I need to do now is to clamp those large lips apart so I can have better access with my hands. You are probably feeling a coldness between your lips. That's a special clamp we use for external exams, unlike a speculum which is used for internals. I'm going to open the lips again, this time with the clamp. There we are. Are you okay?"

"Yes," Carolyn responded.

"Good. Now I'm going to use two of my fingers to pull the hood of your clitoral shaft back. I want to get a good look at the clitoral head to make sure that it's, you know, okay. Yes. Like so. Now I can see it quite well. I must say, you have what I would call a fairly large head under that little hood of yours. Can you feel me touching it? Is it very sensitive?"

"I can feel that a little." Carolyn felt somewhat anxious. What if something was wrong? What if she didn't have any nerve endings there? "Doctor, should I be feeling this a lot more?"

"No, not yet," Dr. Baronson said soothingly, as if she could read Carolyn's mind. "I'm going to apply a little oil to the head now. There. Now I am going to rub up and down on each side of the shaft, like so. Yes. Back and forth in small circles around the head. Do you feel that?"

"Yes," Carolyn murmured, closing her eyes again.

"Very good indeed. Your clitoris seems very healthy as far as sensation is concerned. I am going to continue the massage in order to increase

6

circulation in this area. So often the problem lies there."

And with that Dr. Baronson continued to massage around and across Carolyn's awakened clitoris. With each stroke the surrounding fleshy folds began to swell more and more. Carolyn, lying on the table with her legs spread and lips stretched tightly in the clamp, began to moan quietly. What an incredible experience! What a wonderful doctor to take the time to do such a thorough exam. To care so much. And oh! How good Carolyn was beginning to feel! How hard her clitoris seemed to be! How heavy and full. The tension from the clamps, the coldness of the metal, the constant flicking of Dr. Baronson's finger back and forth over her clitoris.

"Ah, yes," Dr. Baronson was saying. "You swell quite nicely. And you lubricate very well. See? Feel what I am doing." Dr. Baronson slipped her gloved hand down to Carolyn's very damp opening and ran a fingertip around the rim. "As I do this," Dr. Baronson said reassuringly, "as I rim my finger over the entrance to your vagina, I want you to try to clamp down and make the entrance as tight as possible. Yes. Oh, that's very nice. Very nice. You get very wet, very fragrant."

Dr. Baronson was circling her finger around and around as she continued to flick Carolyn's clitoris with the thumb of her other hand. "You seem to respond well, Carolyn. I'd like to open the clamp just a little bit more. Yes. It's going to stretch you a little further apart. Put more tension on the skin around your clitoris. Here we go."

Carolyn felt the clamp spread further, causing her clitoral head to lift, almost ride up another quarter of an inch. The skin was so taut now. So much tension around her clitoris. It almost hurt, yet it felt very good indeed. She was hoping that the doctor would continue. Hoping that the doctor would not realize how hot she was getting.

Christ, she thought. Here I am getting a pelvic exam and I'm so turned on. I suppose that's okay. Only I know it. The doctor is just doing her job.

"Now Carolyn," Dr. Baronson said, interrupting Carolyn's thoughts. "I'm going to insert my fingers into your vagina and I want you to release and then grip my fingers over and over. I need to test the tightness. Your ability to use your inner muscles. Ready? Good. Now I'm entering. That's right. Release. Good. Now tighten. Nice. Very nice. Continue. Open for me. Good. Tighten. Open, tighten. Yes. Very good. You're very tight, Carolyn, I really have to force my fingers in when you tighten down. That's right. Keep it going. Open. Squeeze. Open. Squeeze. As we do this you are going to feel my finger and thumb on each side of your clitoris and I'm going to stroke you in such a way — almost as if I am milking your clitoris. Just so. Good. You may feel some sexual arousal at this point, but that's not unusual. Just relax. This is the only way I can check your responsiveness thoroughly. Very nice."

Dr. Baronson began to move one, then two fingers in and out of Carolyn's vagina. In and out. In and out, simultaneously teasing her very hard, very large clitoral shaft.

Legs stretched, lips clamped apart, Carolyn was beyond herself in pleasure. Never, never had she felt anything like this! The incredible sensation Dr. Baronson was creating by, what did she say,

8

"milking" her clitoris! the intense pleasure each time Dr. Baronson penetrated her as Carolyn alternately tightened and released her vagina!

It was unbearable. Carolyn began to feel out of control. The constant tugging on her clitoris, the tautness of the stretched skin, the penetration slowly in and out — dragging across every fold in her vagina. Milking. Pulling. Kneading. Gripping.

Carolyn felt herself involuntarily arch up — contractions of pleasure shooting through her body. "Oh God! Oh God! Oh God!" She could hear herself yelling far away.

Suddenly, the door slammed open and there stood a matronly woman, perhaps fifty, wearing a white lab coat, a horrified expression on her face.

"What in God's name is going on here, Lydia!"

"Oh, Dr. Baronson!" the blonde-haired receptionist stuttered, pulling her fingers out of Carolyn, standing up, ripping off the lab coat and running out of the room.

Carolyn, stunned and confused, reached down, pulled the clamp from her vaginal lips and covered herself quickly. "What . . . what's going on?"

"That's exactly what I'm going to find out!" replied the angry Dr. Baronson, who turned quickly and stormed out of the room to find the now missing receptionist.

ELYSE

What a city! And such a glorious day! I can't believe I've finally done it! Got on a plane, took myself on a trip, across the country, and got a fabulous room in, if I do say so myself, quite a ritzy hotel. Me, in San Francisco! Definitely the best college graduation present I could have given myself. Twenty-two . . . alone . . . in San Francisco!

Becky was musing to herself, reveling in her independence as she walked slowly through the streets of Chinatown. She had never seen anything like it — the noise, the people, the constant movement. Nothing quite like this in Ohio, nothing quite like this at all.

Walking, window shopping, not paying much attention to this street or that. Just enjoying the warm sun, the blue sky, the sea breeze, the delicious scent of food cooking. Here. There. Down a street, up a street. In a store. Around a corner. Stopping to look in a window. Admiring a jade castle, an ivory Buddha, a beaded necklace, an antique Chinese trunk. Walking, savoring the sights — down one more block, another corner, up a block — turning yet another corner.

Suddenly, Becky was brought out of her haphazard wandering by a man who was calling to her, pulling on her arm, taking her off of her aimless path into a doorway.

"Well, hello sweet lady," he said with a ring of intrigue in his voice. "Come, take a look. See what San Francisco is all about."

Before Becky had a chance to protest, he ushered her into the doorway, pulling a thick red velvet curtain aside. She heard music from somewhere deep within, beckoning, as if calling to her specifically. The entranceway was dark, cool. A tall brunette woman in an ankle-length lace black dress immediately came up to the man. Her smiling lips were tinted red. Dark, lined eyes.

"I . . ." Becky tried to respond. Being piloted so quickly from the bright light outside into the dark entranceway was confusing, disorienting.

"First time here, honey?" the woman said quickly. "You haven't seen San Francisco until you've seen the show at the Thunderbird. Take a look — Elyse is preparing to dance right this very moment."

11

The perfumed woman put her hand against Becky's arm and slightly pushed her forward through yet another set of curtains. Deeper into the club, the tables were illuminated by a dim glow from wall sconces; thick red curtains were pulled back to each side of the stage.

"Here," the woman said, guiding Becky to a table directly in front of the stage. She pulled out the chair, gently forcing Becky into the seat.

"Crystal," the hostess called to a cocktail waitress, "bring our guest here her first drink on me. What's your pleasure?"

"I really don't think I should stay," Becky whispered, somewhat embarrassed. "I've never been in a place like this and I'm not a big drinker . . ." She had been guided into this club, shuffled so quickly to a seat that this was the first chance Becky had to evaluate her situation, let alone respond.

"Crystal, the young lady would do just fine with some nice warm brandy." The woman handed the waitress a five-dollar bill and returned her attention to Becky.

"Look, this will be quite a show. Elyse is the best erotic dancer in town. Give yourself a treat. Do something different! Take a chance!" She gave Becky's shoulder a squeeze and walked away.

Within seconds, Crystal returned, placing a large glass of brandy in front of Becky. "Enjoy the show," she murmured as she turned and disappeared into the darkness.

Still feeling overwhelmed by the briskness, the pushiness of the people who had led her into this club, Becky took a deep breath and looked around.

Well, why not? she thought, once again feeling

that earlier rush of independence, of maturity. She glanced toward the stage. And there, directly in front of her, Elyse was turning — walking gracefully to the left, then to the right. Her sequined jade green dress sparkled as a soft spotlight from the back of the room surrounded her. Moving this way, moving that way, she paraded across the stage, showing off her full breasts that were tucked into her dress. She turned, running her hands across her rounded backside, exhibiting herself, displaying her beauty.

Becky took a sip of the warm brandy. It felt good — burning, forcing its way into her throat. Down, down. Hot, tingling.

The music was coaxing her to relax. The brandy was delicious — a nice sensation. Becky brought the glass back to her moist lips — another sip, another, perhaps another. She felt wonderful, even more at ease. A warmth crept through her body as she watched Elyse who was turning, her full lips smiling, pouting, taunting.

Another sip. And yet another. Becky felt herself slide back into the chair. God! She felt *so* good. *So* comfortable. And that Elyse! The green sequins seemed to dance, to jump into the lights. And her body! How constricted it seemed in that tight, form-fitting dress.

Is Elyse looking right at me? Becky thought, feeling even more relaxed as the brandy's warmth continued to move through her body. Normally, the very idea of Elyse staring at her would have been unsettling, but at this moment, with the safety of the alcohol, the darkness, the music . . . Well, she felt okay that Elyse was staring. And perhaps even okay that she was looking back directly at Elyse.

13

Elyse slid her tongue out from between her thick red lips — and quite deliberately let it journey the length of her upper lip, then her lower lip. Still eyeing Becky, she slowly began to unzip the zipper that began at the top of her dress — directly between her large, plentiful breasts.

Slowly, very slowly, she pulled the zipper down, down, down. Becky was surprised to find how fascinated she was, watching Elyse's painted red fingernails tugging gently on the zipper. Too slowly, Becky thought anxiously. *Too* slowly.

She was engrossed, riveted to that little zipper that was being pulled, dragged so slowly, down past the breasts.

Becky felt herself take a sharp intake of air. Her body was so relaxed and yet so tight at the same time. It was an odd sensation — a pleasurable paradox — on edge, yet floating.

Becky had never seen anything like this. She was entranced, captivated, unable to pull her gaze from that silver zipper that glimmered each time the light hit it just so. Elyse urged the zipper teeth apart, exposing more of the cream-colored breasts. The music rhythmic. Marvin Gaye's seductive voice sensually pleaded for sexual healing as the lights dimmed to a precise red spotlight. Elyse, moving her hands away from the zipper exactly in time to the music, gently drew the jade sequined dress apart just enough, barely enough to show more of those luscious, luscious breasts.

Becky felt overcome with a sudden sensation of heat. Lifting the glass to her mouth, she took another sip as though believing that the brandy, being a liquid, would be the very thing to cool her off, to douse that fire within her.

Elyse was still watching Becky. Only Becky. Were there others in the room? Becky could not, dared not turn her head away from Elyse. It was almost as if Elyse was demanding Becky's full attention, almost as if she was letting Becky know that yes, it was just the two of them. There was no need to turn, to pull away, to separate from each other. Elyse was making her claim — this dance was just Becky, just Elyse.

Elyse turned away and began to let the dress slip off her shoulders — sliding, flowing down her back, smoothly draping over her small wrists, her curved hips, and then lightly dropping to the floor.

The tight emerald-green string from her bikini top stretched across her back and a triangular sequined patch of material barely covered her beautiful rounded ass.

Turn around, please turn! Becky thought fiercely. And, as if in acknowledgment, Elyse slowly glided in time to the music and turned to Becky.

You and me, my darling, her eyes suggested as she faced Becky.

Becky was stunned, mesmerized by what she saw as Elyse danced above her on the stage: those incredible breasts hardly covered by the sequined top, Elyse's womanhood barely hidden by the triangular G-string.

Becky was breathing deeply. Her body felt tight. If only Elyse would let her see those breasts! Were the areolas large or small? Were the nipples rose? Tawny? Will they be hard? Becky felt a stirring between her own legs call to her. She shifted in her seat — as she

15

moved, she could feel the dampness on her panties. Slippery. Wet.

Elyse seemed to watch Becky *so* carefully — perhaps trying to stay in tune with each need Becky had, anticipating her desire and then delighting in satisfying it.

The top? Elyse was most probably thinking. *You're ready for the top now aren't you, my lovely.* Elyse unfastened a tiny hook between her breasts and teasingly, tauntingly, pulled the bikini away, exposing her breasts, once and for all, to Becky.

And there before her, Elyse gave her just what she had been hoping, begging for.

Those breasts — the areolas had a definite rose tint to them — were large, with impressively hard nipples — pert, taut.

Becky felt a sudden aching deep within her vagina. Her clitoris was beginning to throb — her own nipples hardened and alert against the lace of her bra.

Elyse was cupping a breast in one hand — and tugging, pulling, pinching the erect, eraser-like nipple between those deep red fingernails.

Becky shifted again to cross her legs, and was surprised to find that by leaning over, just slightly, and pressing her legs together — leaning and pressing, barely rocking — she could massage her clitoris. Lean and press. Lean and press. She held onto the table, allowing herself an even better angle, a bit more pressure.

And Elyse! Oh, what she was doing to her nipples! So hard, how they stood at attention, now a deep red from Elyse's constant squeezing and twisting!

My God! Becky thought. Now what was she doing? Was that a clamp in her hand? Yes, a small gold clamp with a thin gold chain attached to it. And she was circling the clamp around and around her nipple, causing that large areola to tighten and shrink to barely the size of a dime. Now she opened the clamp, putting her nipple in the mouth of the gold piece.

And now she was tugging that gold chain and moving her hips very slowly — hypnotically tugging and rocking, tugging and swaying.

Becky's hands grasped the table. She was still pressing and releasing against her swollen clit — faster and faster, not caring who could see her. Of course — it was only she and Elyse!

Still tugging the gold chain, still rotating her curved hips, Elyse did the most amazing thing: she turned, spreading her legs, and bent over, still swaying. Her calves were full, pushed up from the emerald green spiked heels, her thighs tight, ass *so* round . . .

It was too much for Becky. With Elyse bent over in this position, Becky could see the swollen lips of Elyse's pussy on each side of the sequined green G-string. Elyse was pulling the sides of the G-string higher and higher on her hips as she moved, slithered, her high round ass. And this lifting of the G-string resulted in the material knotting almost into a thick cord, pushing up, tightly, very tightly indeed between those plush, plump lips of Elyse's pussy.

And Becky was *so* close to the stage that she could, yes definitely, she could take in the scent Elyse was emitting — a musky scent, a demanding scent.

Beyond herself, Becky kept rocking, pressing —

17

taking in the sight, the scent. The material forced its way between Elyse's pussy as Elyse continued sliding, scraping the green sequins against those large pink fluted lips.

Out of control, moaning, Becky exploded into orgasm. She grasped the table so hard she knocked over her drink; the sticky warm liquid spilled into her lap. Her body pulsated.

Elyse turned, blowing a kiss — to Becky? To the audience? Becky had no idea. She was dizzy. Beads of sweat dripped across her brow, down her neck. The thick red curtains were closing. Elyse disappeared behind them.

Becky forced herself up. Staggering, stumbling, knocking against tables and chairs — "Oh excuse, please excuse me . . ." — toward the light at the back of the room, toward the doorway she had been escorted through so long ago. People were talking, ordering drinks, waiting for the next dancer. Becky needed to get out. To the sun. To the street. Past Crystal and the tall brunette at the door. In a hurry. Wanting desperately to get out.

"I told you you'd enjoy the show," the brunette whispered, forcing something into Becky's hand as she pushed past.

Finally she was out the door, into the street. Blinded by the light, she staggered. So very high, soaring — yet she was embarrassed, overwhelmed. Promising herself to erase this whole thing from memory — no one would ever know — she vowed to forget.

Trying to calm herself, taking in a slow, deep breath, Becky suddenly became aware of something softly scratching her palm. Glancing down, opening

18

her tightly clenched fist, Becky was stunned to see the emerald green G-string, sparkling in the sunlight.

Becky's first thought was to throw it immediately into a trash can or the alley — anywhere — just to get rid of it quickly. But instead, without even a second thought, she brought the G-string to her mouth and let her tongue run over its very damp, fragrant center.

JULIA

Julia had completed her training in massage school less than one year ago, and took great pride in how fast she had built her business and how busy her schedule was becoming. It had started slowly, at first, and Julia had seriously wondered if she would ever be able to actually support herself as a masseuse. But recently she had been getting more and more referrals. One client in particular, Mrs. Lindall, had been most impressed and had sent over at least five of her friends for Julia's services.

And now, perhaps Mrs. Lindall had done her the

biggest favor yet. Julia had just hung up the phone after a most intriguing conversation from Laura, Mrs. Christina Huntington's personal secretary. Mrs. Lindall was the interior decorator at the Huntington estate and last week, during a consultation, she had raved about Julia to Mrs. Huntington. And was there any way possible that Julia could fit Mrs. Huntington into her schedule this afternoon?

Julia, without hesitation, had arranged a 2:00 p.m. appointment for Mrs. Huntington, knowing full well that she would have to shuffle the three people she had originally planned to see that day. They could wait. Mrs. Huntington, better known as Mrs. Jonathan Huntington III, was too important a referral to turn down. This could be Julia's golden opportunity to connect with the wealthy upper crust.

The chauffeured limousine was due to arrive within the hour. Julia gathered her portable massage table, the cassette player and tapes, the bag of scented massage oils, and, most importantly, a handful of her business cards. Double-checking to make sure she had everything she needed, she sat down to wait.

An hour later Julia was seated in the back of the limousine. She leaned back in the luxurious seat with a sigh, glancing out the tinted window as the car pulled through the elaborate wrought-iron gates that protected Mrs. Huntington's property.

The possibilities were endless, Julia thought, trying to remain calm, trying not to get too far ahead of herself. Who knew? Perhaps Mrs. Huntington would hire her on a permanent basis. When her secretary called, she had mentioned that Mrs. Huntington had been searching for quite a while for

21

the right masseuse, with no luck. Mrs. Lindall must have said wonderful things about Julia's capabilities because the secretary asked if seventy-five dollars would be enough for an hour and a half. For the "bother" of coming all the way out to the Huntington estate. Julia's normal fee was thirty dollars an hour, and here she was offered seventy-five! If Mrs. Huntington was pleased she might also tell her friends. This was just the break Julia had been praying for! Perhaps she'd even treat herself to that antique lace dress she had been coveting for the last month.

The quick halt of the car brought Julia out of her daydreams. The chauffeur opened her door.

Julia reached out, placing her cool, small hand into his large, warm palm.

"Thank you," Julia said, watching him move to the back of the limousine, open the trunk and pull out her massage table and bags.

"I'll have this set up for you immediately," he said with a quick smile.

Julia took a deep breath and walked up the three low steps that led to a wide veranda. She had barely reached the door when it swung open.

"Good morning," a dark-skinned, attractive woman in a tight-fitting maid's uniform said curtly. "Mrs. Huntington has been anticipating your arrival. Please follow me."

Julia followed the rather stuffy woman into a side parlor. There, on the divan, sat one of the most striking women Julia had ever seen. Mrs. Huntington wore a forest-green silk jumpsuit to complement her long auburn hair and vibrant green eyes. Julia could hardly keep from staring.

Mrs. Huntington stood up and, as gracefully as a doe, walked slowly toward Julia, one hand reaching out in warm greeting.

Julia couldn't move. Mesmerized, she watched this marvelous beauty float toward her.

"I have heard such wonderful things about your work, Julia. I am so pleased to meet you," she said smoothly, her voice a soft symphony of sound. Gently she took Julia's hand into her own.

Mrs. Huntington's skin was a silken contrast to the rugged warmth of the handsome chauffeur's. So delicate! So light! And yet, Julia felt an intense burning travel throughout her body just from the very touch of that exquisite, unassuming hand.

"I've had Michael set your things in the study. Nanette will show you the way. And in the meantime, I'll slip on a robe and join you momentarily."

Mrs. Huntington smiled politely and gave Julia's hand a slight squeeze.

Julia, still tingling from the tender yet electrifying touch of Mrs. Huntington's hand, barely heard Nanette asking her to follow.

"The study?" Nanette said abruptly.

Julia turned, slightly embarrassed, and followed Nanette down the hall to Mrs. Huntington's study. Seeing that her table had already been set up, Julia removed the array of scented oils, cassette player and tapes, a small pillow, and a fluffy, large towel from her bag.

Mrs. Huntington entered wrapped in a thick, blue

terrycloth robe. Her beautiful hair was now pulled back from her face, creating even more emphasis on her finely chiseled features, her emerald green eyes, her cream-colored face lightly dusted with freckles, her barely blushed lips.

"I am so looking forward to this," Mrs. Huntington said softly, almost purring. "I've heard that you are the best masseuse. I suppose Laura, my secretary, told you how I've been searching for a good masseuse. They're so difficult to find — I mean one who knows what she's doing. I get so . . . well, I suppose the word would be tense, on edge, at times and Jonathan has told me over and over that a good massage will relieve all that. I've tried three, no, four different masseuses over the last month. I never can seem to relax, even during the massage —"

"I try to relax my clients initially," Julia interrupted, unable to look at Mrs. Huntington directly, concentrating on the line of her aristocratic nose, the sprinkle of freckles. "If you feel tense after the first few minutes, please let me know. We can work together on this."

Mrs. Huntington smiled.

"There's a towel on the table. Please lie down, face up," Julia continued, turning to the cassette player. She put a tape in, acting as if she was simply doing a menial task, preparing for just another client. Yet her whole being was struggling, fighting an overwhelming urge to turn and watch Mrs. Huntington drop the robe, to sneak a glance, to slyly steal a look at what Julia imagined was a most alluring body.

What am I thinking, Julia chided herself, rather perplexed. This was a client, a *woman* client, whom

24

she was having these feelings toward. What in heaven's name could have gotten into her?

Julia realized that the rustling sound of Mrs. Huntington disrobing and climbing onto the table had subsided. She felt safe in turning to look at Mrs. Huntington, who was lying face up on the table, the towel draped from her mid-chest down and barely over her thighs. Julia pushed the play button on the cassette; a light melody gently filled the room.

For the first time in her professional career she felt awkward, somewhat unsure of herself. Normally, she began at the shoulders, to help the client relax and become accustomed to her touch. But this time, the shoulders didn't seem quite right, and Julia found herself at Mrs. Huntington's long, slender feet. Gently she lifted the right foot and began to apply the viscous oil to her arch. Using a slight pressure, mostly from her thumbs, Julia began to knead the oil into the foot, each time allowing her stroke to become a bit longer, including first the heel, then the ankle and finally working her way clear up to the knee. Kneading and pushing, gradually adding more oil to keep her stroke fluid, smooth.

And all the while that Julia was pushing her hands across the doe-like foot, up the elegant leg, she kept her eyes glued to the towel that seemed to edge its way up just a bit higher on Mrs. Huntington's firm, curved thighs.

Julia customarily concentrated on breathing into the massage until her breath became one with her movement. But today she was having an exceptionally difficult time with her natural deep breathing. Each time she pushed her way up the leg — to the ankle, then exploring a bit further to the calf, then cleverly up to the knee, creeping her way, even stealing her way up onto the luscious, satiny thigh — she found that her breath refused to remain steady. In fact she was panting, as if her breath were in cahoots with her rebellious eyes that refused to pull away from the border of the towel that had lifted even higher.

Julia found herself trembling. She wasn't sure, but for a second, a mere second, when she pushed that last stroke up, about mid-thigh on Mrs. Huntington, she thought she could see, just a small way up under the towel, between Mrs. Huntington's legs. Did she imagine that she had been afforded a brief glimpse of the dark tuft of hair that protected Mrs. Huntington's sex?

As if attempting to disguise her secret motive, she began to pull the leg, ever so slightly to the left each time she moved her hands back down from the full thigh to the ankle — a half inch this time, another half inch. She was so sly, so professional, as though she were giving just a simple massage. Up the leg and slowly down again, she eased that leg from its beginning parallel position to an inviting openness. As if it were an accomplice in this splendidly sneaky undertaking, the towel inched its way further and further up those perfect thighs. Her hands and the towel were partners in a wonderfully executed crime! Julia was able to see directly up the towel to Mrs. Huntington's secret softness.

Mrs. Huntington's eyes were closed; she seemed almost entranced, if not in a delicious dream.

Managing to keep one hand massaging the relaxed foot, Julia was able to reach to her right and angle the small desk lamp directly toward the dark triangle that peeked from under the towel. Just a bit of light, thought Julia, to help me with my massage of course, nothing more.

The light aimed directly at the auburn pocket of fur. Mrs. Huntington's eyes were still closed, her breathing soft, deep, relaxed. Julia palmed the thick oil across the other foot. Kneading her fingers into the soft skin, slowly moving up the defenseless leg, Julia cleverly inched the leg to the right with each stroke, causing Mrs. Huntington's legs to actually be spread quite a bit apart. The beam of light found its way up under that traitor of a towel. Kneading, moving her hands higher, higher to the knee, the thigh, Julia pushed then pulled the sinewy muscles beneath the silky skin. But suddenly, her hands began to rebel as if to say, "No! No more of this! We want more." And as if they were no longer directed by Julia herself, the hands moved higher, using the little finger as a scout, imploring it to hunt its way up to that alarmingly seductive patch of scented hair. Stealthily, it crept to the very edge of the hair — her hands masquerading as healers, as massage tools, while that little finger prowled its way into the forest, gently pulling apart the folds of skin.

And then, to her fortunate surprise, Julia, with the help of that ferreting little finger, was able to see buried between the thick lips, the pinkest peak of tissue that she had ever seen. Like a small, mountainous flap, Mrs. Huntington's clitoral shaft was directly in view. So different in comparison to Julia's own small shaft that she sometimes investigated with a hand mirror when she masturbated.

Mrs. Huntington's treasure rose to a point, and at the tip of that little mountain of skin was a hard

27

gem-like protrusion that jutted out with the gentlest
tugging of the lip by Julia's thief of a little finger.
She moved closer for a better view, still haphazardly
running her other hand over Mrs. Huntington's
shoulder just to keep the pretense, the illusion of the
massage. Julia watched as that insurgent finger
slipped into the valley between that pink mountain
and the dark forest lip — into the glossy cavern,
buttery in its oily thickness — walking like a soldier
into the furry folds, then stealing down to the
elastic-like rim of the rosy pouting mouth.

Massaging the shoulder, across the upper chest,
tugging gently that ally of a towel, Julia worked
down the breast to expose the very border of the
deep red skin of Mrs. Huntington's areola. That little
finger circled very lightly, so as not to be noticed, not
to be a cause for suspicion, around the very inside of
Mrs. Huntington's musky perfumed womanhood.

Peeking at the nipples as the towel flicked over
them with each deep breath Mrs. Huntington took,
Julia glanced back to where her finger had slipped
into that ruby orifice, then to the nipples, now erect
from that rough towel edge, then back to that
oiled-up slit.

Julia could no longer contain the urge to glide her
finger into that oil and then slide it, carefully, slowly
back up to that dangerously hard gem nestled in the
center of that fleshy mountain between Mrs.
Huntington's fat lips. And once there, she allowed her
index finger the luxury of rubbing that little bead of
a clit back and forth in the slippery oil, over and
over. No longer massaging the shoulder, Julia used
her other hand to pull apart those lips — to permit
her full access. Quickly strumming her finger back

28

and forth across the startlingly hard clitoral shaft, she spread the lips as far as possible, stretching the skin, exposing that ripe red clitoral head once and for all.

Barely able to contain herself, Julia once again glanced up to Mrs. Huntington whose eyes were still closed, whose breathing was still deep, sleep-like.

How much Julia had gotten away with! What a stroke of luck that Mrs. Huntington had fallen asleep.

Julia's attention drifted back to those fur-lined lips, that creamy wedge of flesh taunting her to come closer. And with one more quick glance to confirm that Mrs. Huntington was indeed asleep, Julia carefully placed her tongue down into that warm slick slit.

Julia, having never been so close to a woman's vagina before, was overwhelmed by the mysterious spice-like fragrance. As she finally allowed just the tip of her tongue to glaze the hardened miniature rod under the thick spongy flesh, she was surprised to find how sweet the actual taste was. She moved her face closer, gliding her tongue down from those luscious, ample lips to the source of that tangy lubricant. She pushed her tongue against the small cover of skin that protected the entrance of the vagina. It was thick, hard, like a small trap door that stood guard over the secret portal.

Once again, dipping her tongue, she tried to force the tip into a point so it could burrow itself even deeper into that slippery well.

Julia paused. Mrs. Huntington did not move. Her breathing was still deep, regular. Again, she dipped her tongue even farther, pushing her nose right between those plentiful lips. She could barely breathe,

29

immersed as she was, sinking her tongue, increasing the pace just a bit, once again plunging even deeper, pressing her nose into that meaty tissue, the tip of her nose rubbing that glistening, greasy clitoral head. Her face wet, soaked with juices, Julia had never experienced anything quite so exciting.

Quickly, unable to lift her head, no longer glancing up to check Mrs. Huntington, Julia forced her hand into her pants, under her panties which were soaked with her own slippery dew.

Hurriedly she began to work over her own compressed clitoris and continued lapping that incredible slit of Mrs. Huntington's that seemed to grab Julia's tongue and squeeze it even further in.

Licking and tonguing, slapping into that hot splash pool, simultaneously wildly whipping her own small clitoris back and forth until finally, losing herself altogether, she launched into the most intense orgasm she had ever experienced. Satiated, seeing stars, her clitoris still throbbing, Julia collapsed onto the floor, her face drenched with Mrs. Huntington's sweet oils.

Was it seconds, minutes? Julia wasn't quite sure . . . She heard Nanette calling to her, waking her out of her stupor, imploring her to please get off the floor right this minute.

Snapping back to reality with a jolt, Julia suddenly realized her exact circumstances and without opening her eyes she covered her face in her hands and began to cry.

"I'm so sorry. I don't know what came over me . . . Oh! My God! I don't know . . . I can't . . ."

"Please, Miss Julia," Nanette said coolly, professionally. "Mrs. Huntington has ordered the car

30

to take you home. Michael is waiting. We've already packed your belongings. It's time for you to go. Please!"

Julia rose, light-headed, unable to face Nanette, wanting only to cover her face, to run out of the room.

"I suppose you are quite happy with yourself!" Nanette said briskly, stuffing an envelope in Julia's hand and then leading her to the door. Julia, humiliated, stumbled out into the bright sunlight.

The chauffeur, who had already opened the door for Julia, reached for her hand once again and guided her into the seat.

They pulled away from the massive home. "The cream-colored envelope means you're hired," Michael said, looking at Julia through the rear-view mirror. "If she doesn't like you you're handed a check. A cream envelope means there's cash and a note offering you a permanent position."

Julia, still stunned, was barely able to understand the chauffeur's words.

"It's okay," he said, turning and giving Julia a smile. "She went through twelve chauffeurs until she hired me permanently . . . It's all in that initial meeting, you know what I mean?" He gave Julia a wink and turned back to watch the road.

GINGER

Randy leaned her head back, allowing the sun's warm rays better access to her already freckled face. It felt so good lying in the sun, just soaking in the heat. Closing her eyes, she haphazardly dipped her finger into her cool drink and slowly applied the moisture to her parched lips.

Daydreaming, Randy shifted in the chair, taking in a slow, deep breath. Images passed through her mind and then disappeared, leaving her refreshingly blank. She dozed for a few minutes until the heat reminded her of the tall, cool glass of lemonade in her hand.

Her lips once again felt desperately dry. Randy wet her finger and gently brushed the lemonade against them. "Mmmm . . ." she sighed, quietly savoring the sugary liquid as she slowly allowed her tongue to follow its trail of nectar around the periphery of her full rose lips.

It was a sensuous combination — the unrelenting sun, the unexpected coolness of the liquid on her lips, the tingling on her tongue as beads of lemonade soaked into each taste bud.

Randy looked briefly around the yard, shielding her eyes against the sun's glare. "No one home. No one due here for . . ." She glanced down at her watch that she had tossed aside. It would be at least a half an hour before Ginger arrived to pick up the project notes.

"Ah Ginger . . ." Randy closed her eyes once again.

Working side by side on this job with Ginger had been difficult, to say the least. More like unbearable! Ginger — married to that ex-football player, mother of two little girls — was so out of reach. Yet there had been times, working late at the office, just the two of them . . . Ginger across the room, feet propped on the desk, black hair pulled back, pencil in her mouth . . . There was a look in her eye, as if she were secretly implying, covertly trying to signal Randy, that none of it mattered — not the husband, not the marriage — that concealed under this facade was a woman who dangerously desired Randy.

Or perhaps this was all Randy's imagination. After all, Ginger was married and never even once hinted that there was any possibility . . . Yet those eyes beckoned with their seemingly suggestive secrets.

33

Ginger with the long black hair that fell into curls around her beautiful face — the thick eyelashes, clear blue eyes . . . Her pale porcelain-like skin and slender neck that led down to her full womanly breasts . . . Those round hips, that curved feminine ass . . .

These thoughts of Ginger caused a slight tingling sensation between Randy's legs. Again, she opened her eyes and glanced around the yard, satisfied that no one was present. She slowly pulled her bikini bottom down her legs and then let it drop onto the grass, directly on top of her watch.

She leaned back, allowing her legs to spread just enough for the sun's warm finger-like rays to touch her suddenly exposed vulva. Oh! And it felt so nice! The heat of the sun directly on her hidden folds of skin was deliciously stimulating. She sat like this a few moments until that tender skin became so hot that she could literally feel beads of sweat welling up and then dribbling millimeter by millimeter down each side of her clitoris.

She dipped her finger into the lemonade, but this time brought her sugar-laden finger down between her legs, letting the drop of lemonade fall directly onto the top of her clitoral shaft. Her body involuntarily jerked in response to the icy droplet. Randy let her legs fall further apart. The lemonade quickly began to warm. Was she imagining the slight sensation, almost as if the lemonade were sizzling as it evaporated?

Fascinated, she let another drop of lemonade trickle from her finger onto her clitoris, but this time she did not move her finger away. This time she spread the cool liquid around every single crevice between her swollen vaginal lips.

What an incredibly exciting feeling! She dipped two fingers into her drink and allowed them — one on each side of her clitoral shaft — to deposit a trail of lemonade down from the top of the shaft, all the way to her rather moist opening.

Her fingers lingered around the entrance, slowly tracing the slightly raised skin around the rim of her vagina. Almost as if by accident, Randy let one finger dip ever so slightly inside. She swirled it around lightly, then quickly brought her finger to her mouth, placing the mixture of sweet lemonade and her even sweeter juices onto her lips. She delighted in that intoxicating blend of intermingled tastes and fragrances. Randy reveled in them, her senses now quite alert.

Her legs fell even further apart and she trickled several more drops into her secret folds. The lemonade quickly evaporated from her delicate tissue — a light bubbling sensation as the liquid vaporized. She moaned as she felt the sun's heat palpate her hot, sticky womanhood. Slowly she moved her index finger down to the silken skin.

She plunged three fingers back into the lemonade and sloshed the liquid onto her hot, waiting pussy.

The sudden coolness was startling, causing her hips to lift slightly from the lounge chair. Almost immediately she could feel that now familiar effervescence on her honey-sweet pussy. Without a thought, Randy lightly brushed her candy-hard clit. Just a gentle flick, barely touching it really, but enough so that she could feel how that usually spongy shaft had tightened. She submerged her finger into the lemonade and specifically moistened that jujube-like protrusion with one large drop of liquid. Now she granted her finger the reward it so wanted — a slight tap with her finger directly onto the tip of that small nugget. Slowly, she began to stroke back and forth, over and over.

The sun beat down on her sticky clefted hollow — a blend of lemonade and her own candied sap had created quite a lubrication.

As Randy continued the light fluttering on her now distended clitoris, she began a second time to create an image of the very tempting Ginger. Ginger standing in front of her, unbuttoning her blouse; Ginger unhooking her lacy pink bra, exposing her breasts, the nipples hardening even though the air was quite warm . . .

Randy continued her ritual of pleasure, alternately dipping her fingers into the cool lemonade and eagerly back to her thirsty pussy. Flicking, then rubbing and finally beating, yes, beating down on her plump erect clit.

. . . Ginger was lifting her skirt, pulling down the pink panties. Ginger straddled the lounge chair, placing her own swollen pussy directly above Randy's face — spreading herself, pulling the skin back, exposing her ballooned-out clitoral head . . .

Into the lemonade, back to her succulent pussy, Randy drummed harder, faster, more determined, more persistent.

Clenching her eyes tightly, Randy arched her pelvis up from the chair and thrummed feverishly, faster. The frenzy finally ignited into orgasm as she moaned Ginger's name again and again and again.

Panting, she collapsed against the chair, her body hot, flushed, exhausted from pleasure.

Randy, eyes still closed, lifted the glass to her lips and took a sip. The lemonade had the distinct flavor of her own sweet juice.

"Hello."

Randy, startled, forced her eyes open and grabbed her towel in one movement. Embarrassed, she covered her very wet, sticky, exposed pussy.

"I rang the bell and assumed you were out here when no one answered," Ginger continued, the tone of her voice unusually direct. "I hope you don't mind that I took the liberty to come around to the back . . . and interrupt your . . . sun bathing."

"I . . . I . . ." Randy stammered.

"Hot out here, huh." Ginger said, walking up to the lounge chair, leaning over and picking up the sticky glass of lemonade.

"You wouldn't mind if I just wet my own lips, would you?" And with that, Ginger dipped her fingers into the glass and smeared the cool liquid into her mouth.

MISS LAVENDER

When I was growing up, well, things were a lot different then. My mom worked, even though most of my friends' moms stayed home. Daddy had gone to the store one night and never came home, and after that day Mom started working at the five and dime downtown. I was eleven and in my opinion old enough to come home from school and tend to myself. But Mom, she didn't feel comfortable with that, and so that's when Miss Lavender started coming to the house. That's not her real name; in fact, I can't remember what it was — maybe Naomi or Nanette —

but she used to wear this scent of lavender so Mom and I called her Miss Lavender.

I remember the first day she arrived. Standing on the front porch with a flower print dress and a large, floppy straw hat. A yellow hat with some artificial flowers stuck in the brim.

Mom opened the door and as soon as Miss Lavender walked in, the room filled with springtime. Really. She walked like a warm breeze. There was something about her smile, her sparkling eyes that reminded me of Miss Thompson's field way out in the country. All the yellow, white and purple flowers everywhere. Birds chirping, sunshine.

She walked right over to me, extending her hand as if I were some sort of a lady or something and she said sweetly, "So you're Elizabeth!" I don't know quite what happened, except I think the word swoon describes what I felt when she took my hand in hers.

I had never had that kind of feeling before — just kind of dizzy, and praying that Miss Lavender would never ever let go. Her hand was so smooth and warm, and oh that lavender perfume!

Mom talked to her for quite a while, and I sat there in the corner pretending to play with my dolls, real quiet, so Mom wouldn't make me leave the room. I sat there, holding my dolls as if I was absorbed in some sort of important game, but all the while I was asking God to let her stay.

God answered me, 'cause Miss Lavender started coming to my house every day. Mom worked from 1:00 PM to 9:00 PM so Miss Lavender would get there before I got home from school and would stay till 9:30 cleaning up, cooking dinner, doing household chores for Mom.

Sometimes, when I'd get home from school, Miss Lavender would be in the middle of cleaning the kitchen. That was always my favorite activity of hers — she'd climb up on a stool to wash down the cabinets. I used to watch her body as she stretched to reach the top cabinets. I'd sit in the corner, eating a cookie and sipping some ice-cold milk that Miss Lavender had poured for me, and I'd watch and watch.

Miss Lavender used to bake cookies on Wednesdays. She'd wait for me to come home and then we'd mix the batter together. I'd beg for a taste and I'd ask her over and over, "Please let me lick the spoon. Please, please." And she'd shake her head. That is, until all the chocolate chips had been added. Then she'd say: "Is my sugar ready for some sugar?" And I'd get so excited 'cause I knew she was going to let me taste the batter with those big chunks of chocolate. But the best part of all was that she'd dip her finger deep into the sticky batter — twirl it around, it seemed like forever and then would let me lick the delicious paste off her finger.

Oh Miss Lavender! Such good memories. She seemed so sophisticated, so sure of herself. I thought she was a real lady with all those flowered dresses and hats and beaded purses. Once, when I had fallen on Mr. Goober's porch, she even took a lace hanky from her purse and dabbed my eyes. That's a lady! I used to dream about Miss Lavender at night. She and I on a bus going far away, maybe out to Miss Thompson's house with the flowers. Then I'd wake up and be sad to find myself alone in my bed.

That reminds me of the time when Mom went to visit her sick Aunt Tilly and Miss Lavender stayed the night. I was asleep and had oh, I think my worst dream ever, one I still remember to this day. Miss Anderson, my teacher, had a white rabbit and she was going to cut his ear off with a pair of scissors and I was screaming "No! No! No!" Suddenly I woke up, my face covered with tears, and Miss Lavender was holding me, running her hands through my hair saying, "Hush, Hush, sugar, Miss Lavender will take good care of you." Being in her arms, pulled in close to her soft body, surrounded by fresh flowers — well, that's the night I knew for certain I was in love with Miss Lavender.

Mom met a man at Aunt Tilly's. Some sort of a veterinarian. Before I knew it they were talking marriage, and Mom was walking around the house singing. I heard her on the phone to her friends, talking about quitting the five and dime 'cause now that she and Nathan were getting married, she could stay home and raise her daughter right.

That's when I really started praying. Every night I'd get on my knees and pray desperately that God would keep me and Miss Lavender together. I picked up every penny I found, I didn't walk on sidewalk cracks and every night I put my magic rock under my pillow. I was that serious about keeping Miss Lavender around.

But all the praying, all the jumping around over sidewalks, the rock — well, I guess it just wasn't enough — 'cause that horrible day came when Mom told me Miss Lavender was coming back just one last time. I said, "Oh really." Kind of holding back everything. Then I ran up to my room, grabbed my magic rock and cried and cried.

Miss Lavender, that last day, was sad too. I could

41

see it in her eyes. She took me out to the front porch and we sat there on Mom's swing chair and swung back and forth together for maybe two hours. She just put her arm around me, didn't say much, and we rocked. When it was time to go, Miss Lavender told me she was going to New York City to find a new life and she handed me the prettiest necklace. It had a jagged heart dangling from it with the word *Some* engraved on it. Well, I didn't understand it, but I felt such a shiver because I loved that necklace right away. Then she pulled from underneath her flowered neckline a chain with the other half of the heart. She read me the word on hers: *day.*

She leaned over and whispered "Some day when you're older — maybe twenty and I'll be almost thirty-six — you come to New York and look for the other half of your heart." With that she pulled me to her gently and kissed me right on the lips. A kiss like I'd never felt before — I could feel the soft fullness of her lips, a light breeze of lavender and honeysuckle just about filling my whole body, making me think I would float away if I didn't move real close to Miss Lavender. My head was dizzy like I had just got off the merry-go-round at Twin Rock Park . . . and when I felt her lips open just the tiniest bit and a heat of some sort pass right from her mouth into mine, well that sent a tingling through me the likes of which I've never felt since. And for just the quickest second, Miss Lavender let her warm tongue softly move into my mouth . . . Like honey and sugar all mixed together, that's how my Miss Lavender tasted. Then she pulled away. Wiped a tear from her eye and said we should be going on over to Dr.

42

Nathan's now. And that's just what we did. Oh, Miss
Lavender . . .

Nadine wearily fell into the hard padded seat and
let out a moan. The subway car as usual was jammed
with people. Friday was always a particularly dreadful
day to travel home from work — she'd been on her
feet all day and now had to compete for a seat not
only with the regular commuters but the weekenders
as well. Almost never did she find a place to sit in
the sardine packed cars. But this evening she
happened to be standing in the right place at the
right moment and when the woman with the
oversized shopping bag moved up and out of a seat,
Nadine managed to steal the sacred space and finally
get off her feet.

Her left foot began to ache insistently. Working
Christmas hours in her Manhattan dress shop was
stressful enough, but today's four-hour special sale,
and that large woman with the spiked heels who
maneuvered in such a way as to spear Nadine's
vulnerable left foot . . . Next year she'd hire extra
help, no question about that! Nadine tilted her head
back, closed her eyes momentarily, and then leaned
forward in an attempt to massage her throbbing foot.

"Excuse me, please?"

Nadine's moment of peace was interrupted by a
rather timid voice above her.

"I'm sorry to bother you, really," the young
woman continued, "but I'm new in town and I think
I'm lost and I really don't know . . . I'm bothering
you, oh I'm so sorry. People in a big city are

frightening sometimes and I don't know, you looked so . . . I'm really sorry . . . I . . ."

"Oh please," Nadine said sincerely, aware of the desperateness in the woman's voice. "I'm glad you asked me for help. You're lost?"

"Well, it's more like I'm not sure where I'm actually headed. There's supposed to be a women's hotel called The Marlin and I thought I was going in the right direction but I'm totally confused now."

"The Marlin!" Nadine said with a smile, thinking back to fifteen years ago when she'd first arrived in New York. Standing in front of The Marlin Hotel, a large flowered satchel filled to the brim, her straw floppy hat being lifted from her head by a warm New York spring breeze. "I know The Marlin quite well."

"Oh! what a relief! Other people, the ones that didn't ignore me, had no idea what I was talking about."

"Well, it looks like you've struck gold. I'm Nadine." She lifted a hand toward the somewhat frazzled-looking woman in a gesture of friendliness.

"I'm Liza," the younger woman replied, letting out a small sigh, and reaching down to clasp Nadine's hand.

Feeling the delicate texture of Liza's hand, Nadine hesitated, and then slowly let her own hand slide out from the light handshake. She allowed her eyes to look directly into Liza's and then said, "We're about two stops from where you'll want to get off. The Marlin's a few blocks or so from there. Have you eaten dinner? There's a wonderful cafe not far from The Marlin that serves the most marvelous hot soups and fresh baked breads — how about joining me for a bite to eat?"

"That sounds absolutely delicious!" Liza said.

"Then it's settled. A woman new to this city needs a friend. Believe me I know," Nadine added.

Liza ran her hand through her short brown hair giving it a quick tousle. "That's exactly what I need right now!" The clouded confusion that had cast a shadow on her face broke into a dazzling smile.

"Good, then a friend is what you've got! We'd better work our way towards the door." Suddenly, Nadine no longer felt burdened by her earlier weariness. Something about Liza, her smile, her innocent sparkling eyes, filled Nadine with a renewed energy. Even her left foot had stopped aching.

"Let me give you a hand with those bags." Nadine grabbed for one of Liza's small suitcases and pushed toward the exit. People crammed together and resenting any further infringement on their already limited space, gave the two women dirty looks as they pried their way out of the subway car and finally into the subway terminal.

Liza, wearing a large brown overcoat, dark brown boots and carrying a tweed suitcase, kept her eyes on Nadine as she followed her up the escalator and out into the New York winter night. And Nadine was certainly something to watch, with her antique fox coat, the beautiful deep purple felt hat which was adorned with a remarkable lizard pin. She walked briskly ahead carrying Liza's other bag as if she had only just arrived at the terminal moments before, expressly to greet a good friend visiting for the holidays.

Nadine, one hand holding the felt hat from lifting off her head into the brisk wind, flailed with the other hand to catch the attention of passing taxis.

45

Liza wrapped her own coat around her as she watched the wind draw open Nadine's fox coat exposing a hint of a beautiful flowered dress, its violets matching the rich purple of Nadine's felt hat. Nadine was laughing, calling to Liza, "See, this is how! This is how!" Jumping, making faces until a cab driver finally took the dare and zoomed directly over to Nadine.

Within minutes they were climbing out of the cab in front of Mama's Cafe, Nadine digging into her beaded purse for the fare, shooing away Liza's offer to pay, motioning for her to get into the warmth of the restaurant and out of the cold night air. Then Nadine caught up with Liza, taking her soft hand and guiding her toward the back corner booth. The aroma of fresh baked bread was overwhelming.

"I didn't realize how hungry I was!" Liza said eagerly.

Both Nadine and Liza pulled off their coats and slid into the booth. They let out exclamations of pleasure.

"I tell you Liza . . ." Nadine's voice was soft and mysterious. "People are seen coming into this cafe but never coming out . . ."

Liza laughed lightly and then took a moment to allow herself to savor the luscious odors that surrounded her. This restaurant was a welcome relief from the weather, the hours of traveling, the feeling of being lost and alone. Liza glanced across to Nadine and let another smile escape her lips.

Treating herself to warm, thick slices of bread slathered with soft butter and honey, Nadine finally had a chance to observe Liza a bit closer. The brown hair, cut in fluffy layers, outlined her pretty country girl face. She was young, Nadine guessed early twenties or so, with bedazzling eyes and a remarkable smile. A natural beauty, Nadine thought, still surveying Liza who was talking vivaciously about the tribulations of her adventurous day. There was something intriguing about Liza's voice, those eyes that seemed in awe of the world . . .

Her gaze drifted from Liza's face to the forest green crewneck sweater and on even further to the shiny gold necklace where a charm sparkled every time the light hit it just so.

"Interesting," Nadine commented, reaching over the bread to lightly take the jagged half heart charm into her hand. She felt the smoothness of the gold, worn from wearing. "Looks quite old," she said, letting the charm drop against the green backdrop of Liza's sweater and allowing her eyes to move back up to Liza's face to study the woman's features more clearly. "I'm an antique lover — jewelry, furs, hats, you name it — so I always find myself drawn to things from the past." Nadine looked directly into Liza's deep brown eyes. "Such as your lovely heart."

"It was a gift," Liza responded, taking the small heart into her own fingers. "A woman, from years ago, gave it to me as a farewell gift. The most wonderful woman, really . . ."

Letting her mind drift back into memories of the past, Liza began to tell Nadine the story of Miss Lavender — easy to remember, easy to recount. She had detailed the memory for days, then months, and finally years after Miss Lavender had kissed her that last day.

"Oh Miss Lavender . . ." Liza sighed, having finished painting the exquisite portrait of her for

47

Nadine, and still holding the jagged heart between her fingers.

"So, is that why you've come to New York? To find the other half of your heart?" Nadine asked, rather taken by the young woman and her story of Miss Lavender.

"In my fantasies I'll always dream of finding her, that it's a destiny of some sort. But as I said, I don't even know her real name . . . I used to beg Mom to tell me, to try to give me some information, but she always says that's too far back for a woman like her to remember. And I wouldn't even recognize her — after all, it's been over fifteen years."

Liza released the half heart. "So, I'm in New York to try to make something of myself as Mom would say. And if I'm supposed to find Miss Lavender, I reckon it will happen just on its own. But for a little added luck —" Liza leaned over slightly, managing to pull something out of her brown wool pants pocket. "See," she said coyly, "my magic rock."

Liza paused, licking a bit of honey from her finger. "The Midwest is okay for growing up but I'm ready for a challenge. And here I am, and I couldn't even figure out how to get to my lodging!"

"Oh really Liza! I think you've done quite well. One day and you've already found the best cafe, the hotel's only a few blocks away and —"

"And I've found a friend," Liza interrupted. "Thank you so much Nadine, really."

The waitress appeared carrying a tray laden with steaming bowls.

Liza dipped her spoon into the thick pea soup.

She glanced up at Nadine who was buttering another slice of the warm bread.

Nadine was late thirties–early forties, and still very attractive. The small laugh lines barely visible around her eyes were most probably the after-effect of having smiled so fully, so often, over the years. The gentle streaks of silver woven through her thick black hair only enhanced its rich color. Something about Nadine was fresh, forever young, like a spring day, like a walk in a field, a float down the river back home on a hot summer day . . . relaxing, being carried downstream.

"Liza!" Nadine's voice had a light sparkle to it. "Where have you drifted to? Staring out into space sucking on your spoon!"

Embarrassed, Liza pulled herself out of the daydream of Nadine, of childhood memories and of the hot summer sun. "I . . ."

"You must be exhausted," Nadine said with a kindly smile. "I don't want to sound too bold or presumptuous, but why don't you come to my house tonight? Really. There's plenty of time for The Marlin. I've got a big tub I could fill to the brim with bubbles, you could soak forever if you wish and . . . it's a home."

"Nadine," Liza replied happily, "that sounds perfect. I would love to."

And not too much later, contented with good food, warmed by good conversation, the two women wrapped themselves in their coats and prepared once again to brave the winter night.

Nadine again captured the attention of a passing taxi, and the women soon found themselves enclosed

49

in the warmth of a cab and moving quickly through the busy New York streets.

"I can't believe how cold it is tonight!" Liza said, shivering lightly, the cab's heater not yet warming her fully.

Nadine put her arm around Liza, pulling her close. "Is this any better?" she said, noticing how perfectly Liza fit to her own body.

Liza looked at Nadine with a smile and then allowed her head to gently rest on Nadine's shoulder.

"You've had quite a day," Nadine said soothingly, letting her hand move slowly through Liza's windblown hair.

"West Eighty-eighth," the cab driver interrupted.

Liza and Nadine lugged the suitcases up the two flights of stairs to Nadine's flat. Nadine led the way into the most inviting room that Liza had ever seen.

"Just sit," Nadine said quickly, pointing to the large overstuffed antique couch. "I'm going to draw you a bubble bath, light us a fire and then get us both a glass of wine. Sound good?"

"Sounds great!" Liza said, walking over to the couch and sinking into its billowy softness.

The apartment was definitely an extension of Nadine, full of soft antique furnishings embellished with pillows arrayed like a bouquet of spring flowers. An oak hat stand blossoming with straw, felt and fur hats. Flowers in vases on the table, on the mantle. A small porcelain bowl gently cupping a colorful mixture of potpourri on a dark wood coffee table. Liza recognized the dried rosebuds, but was unsure of the deep violet petals. She raised the delicate bowl to her nose, taking in the delightful blend of fragrances.

Interesting photos in antique frames sat on the end table. Liza picked up the larger picture with the silver frame for further examination. A striking woman stared into a mirror, a hand tangled in her dark wavy hair. Liza replaced the picture on the table and reached for a smaller one in a pewter frame. A woman, hair pulled into a bun, was flattening dough with a rolling pin, a small girl at her side.

Liza let out a sigh. This apartment was as comfortable and warm as Nadine was herself. And every part of it, the knickknacks, the pictures, the pastel pillows — all evoked that same feeling that Liza had experienced in the restaurant.

Liza's gaze drifted back to the picture of the woman rolling the dough. Memories, sweet memories of back home years ago with Miss Lavender. The kitchen smelling of butter and sugar. The house always like springtime and flowers, Miss Lavender wiping away her tears, Miss Lavender kissing her that last good-bye . . . Liza reached up and touched the half heart pendant.

"Liza!" Nadine called from down the hall. "I've drawn you the most luxurious bath. It's taken everything I have to keep from getting in myself!"

The bathroom was filled with candlelight from antique light fixtures. A large antique tub stood majestically on bear claws, steam rising above an avalanche of bubbles. Thick fluffy towels hung from a wooden stand. There was a porcelain statue of two women carrying a basketful of flowers, gazing at their reflections in a mirror lake.

And what a vision Nadine was, in a satin flowered robe that partially covered her lilac satin nightgown.

She stood surrounded by a halo of candlelight, enveloped in the fragrance of rosebuds and tulips. Liza felt entranced, caught in a spell.

"You see?" Nadine said, her voice no more than a whisper. "Isn't that bath most tempting?"

Liza returned her gaze to the alluring tub filled to the brim with a snowdrift of perfumed bubbles.

"And if you'd like, after you've soaked for a bit, we could refresh your skin with a loofah scrub . . . I assure you, you will never be the same after you've had your skin polished with one of these treasures from the sea."

Nadine reached over to a small basket balanced on the edge of that marvelous tub. "Here," she said, handing the wiry looking ball to Liza. "Try this on your skin. "I'll get a fire going . . . and if you like the loofah, I'll scrub your back for you in a bit."

Liza took the sponge into her hand, unable to break away from the bewitchment she felt. She did not, could not reply. It was as though she had wandered into an extraordinarily tranquil dream where an enchanting goddess had been awaiting her arrival.

Nadine, as if sensing Liza's state, moved slightly closer and said softly, "Go ahead, it's all yours . . ." She moved past Liza, creating a delicate stirring of fragrances. "I'll be in after awhile to make sure you don't drift into dreamland."

Liza listened to Nadine's light steps down the hall. She took a moment to once again savor the bathroom with its amber glow from the candles. The steam rising from the bath water seemed to emit a floral scent of its own. Letting out a sigh, full of anticipation, Liza tugged off her clothing and walked over to the tub. One touch with the finger . . . water almost too hot . . . one dip of the toe . . . and she was sinking down, down, down deep into the cloud of bubbles. Losing sight of her body, losing the tenseness from her full day of travel. This, right here, was heaven.

Nadine adjusted the log in the fireplace and leaned back appraising the roaring fire. She loved having a fireplace . . . could stare into a fire for hours. She heard the splashing of the bath water. Liza was probably quite relaxed by now.

Still gazing into the dancing flames, Nadine thought back to the small golden half heart that Liza was wearing — the story of Miss Lavender. Amazing the effect a segment in one's life could have, how a person could take a memory and carry it around forever. Revising it, reliving it, making decisions because of it. Like Liza, like herself. Yes, she understood a lot about Liza, more than Liza could ever imagine.

She just wasn't quite sure if what she was considering was in everyone's best interest. Would Liza be happier living with a childhood fantasy? God only knew how hard it was to compete with that. She herself had been through that kind of a situation with Harriet. Dear Harriet who just couldn't let go of her first love Rebecca. Nadine had tried everything to weed that memory from Harriet's heart so there would be adequate space for her own love. But inevitably, the haunting ideal love from Harriet's past had defeated her.

And now lovely Liza, like a ripened fruit ready to be plucked, could be hers if she handled the situation properly. Did she let Liza know the truth about her identity, or did she need to masquerade as someone she was not? It was obvious that *no one* could compete with the "perfect" Miss Lavender from the past. No one. If she admitted to being Miss Lavender there would be the pressure of living up to that childhood memory. But if she acted as though she was just a new person in Liza's life, that would be just as difficult. Either way Nadine knew she would have to wrestle with the Miss Lavender from the past.

She wanted Liza, wanted to own the precious love that seemed to swirl like a flurry of petals afloat in a spring breeze every time Liza spoke of Miss Lavender. Yes. It was time to try once again. Time to take one final risk. She rose from in front of the hypnotic fire and began to slowly wend her way back to the bathroom where, if she was correct in her intuition, Liza would be awaiting her.

Nadine tapped lightly on the partially closed door. "Liza?" she said, her tone delicate. "May I come in?"

"Oh, Nadine," Liza responded, shifting in the tub a bit, turning to face her. "Words can't express how relaxed I feel."

Nadine stepped into the room, it's air saturated with a fragrant dew. "Have you tried the loofah?" she asked. Liza was shoulder deep in bubbles that glimmered faintly in the candlelight.

Liza giggled. "I got into the tub holding that sponge and haven't seen it since!"

"Would you like me to wash your back? That is if you can muster up the energy to find it in there!"

Liza searched the bottom of the tub. "Oh! Here!" she said in such a way that Nadine could not help being more charmed. Liza was like a little girl, so delighted with even the simplest of life's pleasures.

Nadine took a moment to reconsider how she wanted to proceed. Did she dare take the risk? Would Liza accept her? She had sworn after the terrible hurt with Harriet never to open her heart again . . . But there was Liza, the freshest of flowers, so new to the arena of life. Perhaps Liza was exactly what she needed.

Nadine approached the tub and gently took the loofah from Liza's hand. "Lean forward," she said, her voice barely more than a whisper. "I'll scrub your back."

Nadine began to scrub her bubble-covered back, at first not applying much pressure, but then increasing to a medium stroke.

Liza let out a small moan and as Nadine continued the massage she moved in closer to Liza, squatting down next to her, tenderly whispering in Liza's ear.

"Liza, my dear, dear Liza. There is something I've wanted to say to you . . . ever since I first noticed your golden half heart at the restaurant and frankly, I've been torn as to what to do." Nadine paused, continuing to rub the rough sponge across Liza's back, still whispering into her ear. "There are so many chances we take in life . . . sometimes we win, sometimes we lose . . . But with you, dear Liza, I feel like I have no choice but to tell you the truth."

"What is it, Nadine?" Liza said, unable to hide her sudden apprehension.

"Hush, hush now," Nadine said, remembering the story of Miss Lavender, searching for the exact words that would reveal her identity yet would assure Liza at the same time. "No need for alarm, Miss Lavender will take good care of you."

Liza felt an intense shiver move quickly through her body. Stunned, she turned to Nadine and looked into her eyes, then examined her face, still not quite able to respond.

"Yes, Elizabeth, it's me," Nadine said, her words smooth, loving.

"Miss Lavender? Miss Lavender!" Liza said, trembling inside. "I found you, without even looking! God meant it to be, I always knew it. I said it just about every day . . . that God meant it to be and because of that, because God takes care of things just so, I knew I'd find my Miss Lavender!"

"Yes, Sugar, that's exactly right, God meant it to be." Nadine was stroking Liza's hair, kissing her ever so carefully on the cheek, and then finally moving closer until her soft full lips were only a breath away from Liza's own pink mouth. Slowly, Nadine let the tip of her tongue lightly brush the small area between Liza's lips, letting her warm tongue gently part them just a bit more, allowing her to trace the entire peripheral of Liza's sweet lips.

Liza, overwhelmed with emotion, not quite able to come to terms with onrushing events, felt an incredible sensation sweep through her as Nadine caressed her lips. A feeling like she had only felt once before in her life when Miss Lavender had kissed her that final good-bye. One touch from Nadine's tongue and she felt every one of her cells burst into a tingling chain of electrical surges.

Nadine continued to flick her tongue, barely touching Liza's lips . . . not stopping to kiss, not daring to enter Liza's mouth, to connect with Liza's anxiously awaiting tongue.

No. Softly. Gently. She teased her tongue across and around the vermilion borders of those succulent lips. Taking Liza's face into her hands tenderly. Breathing deeply. Moaning, not quite audibly.

Liza, still not recovered from the shock of finding her Miss Lavender, from the intensity of her lips on Liza's, wanted only to swoon. She felt dizzy, unable to breathe.

"Elizabeth," Nadine said, pulling away from Liza and peering deeply into those innocent brown eyes. "May I join you in the bath?"

Liza, not able to speak, nodded. Nadine rose from the tub and began to unwrap her satin robe. She reached over to a brass hook and let the robe drape from it.

Liza watched Nadine, whose back was towards Liza. She looked beautiful, surrounded in a light glow from the candlelight. As in a breeze, the satin gown slipped from Nadine's curved body onto the floor. She leaned towards the mirror, removing a barrette from her hair.

Liza stared, unable to move her eyes from the silhouette of Nadine's enticing round bottom outlined in the candlelight. Leaning, inadvertently pushing up just a bit as she adjusted something on a small shelf, she strained, raising on her tiptoes, causing her gracefully shaped calves to tighten . . . as though they were purposely showing themselves off to Liza. Those particularly rounded hips, so inviting! So womanly! Flowing into her small waist and then flaring out again to her smooth back.

Nadine turned to face Liza saying something

about what a coincidence! What a small world after all! Liza wasn't paying much attention to the words anymore. Miss Lavender was standing in front of her, now completely undressed. Her breasts were soft and feminine, with dark large nipples that decorated their tips.

Nadine floated, or so it seemed, back over to the tub. "Let me slide in behind you," she murmured, carefully stepping into the tub, squeezing herself into the small space that Liza had created for her.

The water, still quite warm, felt soothing to Nadine. She moved cautiously, not wanting to cause Liza to feel any apprehension. She sank into the water, the bubbles rising almost to the edge of the tub. Sliding her legs on each side of Liza and then taking her into her arms as if she were a child, Nadine drew Liza to her. She felt Liza's body respond immediately, as though Liza had been waiting all along to be encircled by, surrounded by, yes . . . even encompassed by Nadine's protecting arms.

"You know, Liza, that it's you and me now. That we've found each other and we'll always be together." Nadine was softly stroking Liza's hair as she spoke, still holding Liza in close to her body.

"Yes, Nadine, yes . . . you are all I want. I just can't believe how lucky I was to find you." Liza leaned back further. She was surprised to find how perfectly she seemed to fit into Nadine.

Nadine closed her eyes, relishing the intimacy. It had been so long since she had held anyone, since she had let anyone come in too close. She had longed for it, craved it, but had no longer been willing to fight the demons from her lovers' pasts that always seemed to intrude in her relationships. But this — this was a most fortunate set of circumstances. That a chance meeting could turn her life around so dramatically! No longer to be afraid of the first love from the past . . . she *was* the first love. No, there would be no regrets for the decision she had made. Liza seemed very willing to accept Miss Lavender as she was today.

Nadine began to caress Liza's back then, bringing her hands slowly down and around to Liza's full breasts. The room was quiet except for the water moving gently as Nadine continued to touch Liza.

Liza let out a soft purr as Nadine cupped her breasts, the hot water and the bubbles in front of Liza swishing in tempo to movements of Nadine's hands.

"You are so lovely," Nadine said breathlessly, gently stroking Liza's unexpectedly generous breasts.

Slowly, she raised the right breast in her hand as she allowed her eager fingers to slide their way down towards the nipple.

Not having yet seen Liza's breasts, Nadine could only imagine what they would look like. She closed her eyes, allowing herself the luxury of trying to create the image of Liza's ripe breast by touch alone. So very shapely! So very soft! And the nipple . . . yes, the nipple — quite large, almost a half inch in its firm erected state, perhaps the shape of an elongated rectangle? So agreeably responsive. So expressive in its pleasure!

Nadine let a soapy finger flick back and forth across the compressed, awakened nub. The areola was tightened, ruffled . . . surrounding the pert nipple like a ballerina's skirt. Probably quite pink, Nadine thought as she continued to finger that large geometrical-shaped pellet ever so slightly, now pushing it into the generous areola, now pulling it back out between her index finger and her thumb.

Liza, her entire body swept up in a deep heat, leaned further into Nadine. Pressing her back against Nadine's soft receptive breasts, wanting only to feel those protruding tips that she had seen as Nadine had dropped the satin gown . . . They had seemed so deep red in the amber light from the candles . . . the nipples so thick, so determined. She only wanted to rub up against them again and again.

And oh! what a tingling, what a creamy feeling Nadine was creating with just the simplest pulling, just the lightest tugging on that remarkable distended nipple. How insistent the throbbing sensation between her own legs was becoming.

"You like that?" Nadine asked as though she had been reading each thought as if formed in Liza's mind.

"Oh yes! Yes!" Liza responded quickly. She had never felt anything that had stirred her so. "Nadine," she continued, shifting slightly in the tub, "I need you to know that I feel an extraordinary closeness to you . . . just from the fact that you are Miss Lavender. Perhaps I've been foolish to be so devoted to a memory, letting it carry me away like this. But being next to you, having your arms around me, your touch . . ."

"Liza, please dear, it's quite all right. We both have the same memories. It's no different for me. Come, let me love you the way I've always dreamed."

Nadine let her hands slowly move from Liza's breasts, exploring the smooth tapered waist. How the texture of Liza's skin was like the finest silk. How like a painting the curve of her waist blossomed into petal-like hips. Nadine took her time, slowly following the feminine slope of Liza's hips and gradually permitting her hands to caress her smooth, rounded belly.

This, this right here is what loving a woman is all about, she thought as she let her hands slide back up to Liza's luscious breasts and then gently let them glide back down the slippery skin, once again over the half moon belly and even further on towards Liza's hidden womanhood.

Lightly at first, just barely brushing over the loosely curled hairs . . . only the fingertips . . . so very carefully, so very lovingly, working their way . . . and oh! right to that perfect place where the triangle of hair divided itself into the liplike folds.

Adeptly, Nadine's finger manipulated, using a light flicking motion to aid her in separating the barely furred little lips. The outer lips were surprisingly small, almost childlike with their light coating of baby fine hair.

Nadine, even more aroused by the curious contradiction of Liza's ample breasts and her diminutive outer lips, did not need encouragement for her demanding finger to continue its investigation deeper between the petite lips. Closing her eyes, trying to create a picture by touch alone of what her eyes would later be rewarded with. Ah! And there it was — simply a hardened flange of tissue. How very sexy! How very, very sexy! Nadine thought, again considering the paradox of the large woman-like breasts and that small pussy.

Liza, letting another moan escape from her lips, was caught in a whirlwind of sexual tension. Nadine's probing finger moving so faintly, barely grazing the area between her legs that ached so! And then how hesitatingly it had parted her lips, how inquisitively it had tapped lightly up and down across her clitoris. As though palpating, as though making some sort of evaluation.

Nadine prompted her finger to tap ever so slightly up and down. Just a simple movement, really, but one that caused Liza's clitoris to tighten up even more. Yes, nudging it, working it, now moving down and dipping past the even smaller inner lips into the secret opening . . . dabbing a fingertip full of the jelly-like oil and sliding it back up and over the now very compressed clit.

Quickly, Nadine began to flap her finger up, over and across, up, over and across the stubby button of a clit.

Liza, crying out in pleasure, quite out of control, begged "Please more! Please faster! Oh please!"

"Liza, my dear, I'm going to make you crazy!" Nadine said, her voice husky from the sexual heat. Hurriedly, she leaned over the side of the tub and pulled a small water massager from the floor and attached the hose end to the faucet.

"Lean back, my lovely," she said, situating herself behind Liza. "Let me hold you while I give you a most extraordinary treat."

Nadine then turned the massager on as Liza placed herself against Nadine's soft breasts. Immediately the water began to pump out of the massager head in a steady rotating stream.

"Spread your legs for me, that's right, let each

one hang over the sides of the tub. Here, I'll hold you up," Nadine coaxed.

Liza, leaning back, propped her legs up and over the sides of the tub.

Nadine took the water massager and directed the flow of water towards that aroused clit that she had been fondling only moments before.

"Ah!" Liza sighed as the first stream of water began to pulsate on her clitoris.

"You direct me. You direct me," Nadine said, quite excited herself.

Liza took Nadine's hand and aimed the water current to the exact place that seemed to be clamoring emphatically for attention. When the squirting water hit its precise goal, Liza arched back, pushing her legs even further apart. Lifting herself, lunging forward now, straining to keep that strong little tide of water directly on her now engorged nugget.

"Yes, Nadine! Yes!" she cried, still angling herself this way, that way, trying to stay right with the bouncing spray of water.

"That's my girl. There she goes," Nadine whispered, still grasping Liza tightly, imagining what that pussy must look like right now with the water forcing the lips apart, with that small iron-like clit hungrily trying to stay in the exact spot, Liza rotating her hips to follow the skipping of the water flow.

Liza's grasp tightened around Nadine's wrist. Still aiming, still zeroing in with that incredibly warm jet stream of water that hurriedly danced on top of her

thickened pink knot of a clit. Over and over, the
water darting, prodding again and again!

Liza's entire body arched into orgasm, her hips
rocking, bubbles splashing up and over the sides of
the tub.

"Oh yes! Oh yes! Oh yes!" Nadine was saying,
holding Liza, holding the massager. "Feel it dance,
feel it pulse!"

Liza was in the throes of the most incredible
sensation, her body stiffened in the deepest of
pleasure, only concentrating on that pulsating stream,
following its subtle movements like slivers of iron
parading after a magnet, only wanting to stay in
direct line with that water forever and ever!

Finally, although it seemed as though the
intensity had gone on for a remarkably long time, she
found it necessary to pull away from the water . . .
satiated, fulfilled.

"Nadine . . ."

Nadine encircled Liza in her arms, drawing her as
close as possible. "Just you and me, forever?"

"Yes, Nadine. Yes." Liza was slowly beginning to
return from the narcotic-like stupor in which the
orgasm had left her. "Nadine, let me try that on you.
You pleased me so .. ."

"Don't you worry my sweet Liza, there's plenty of
time for my pleasure. In fact, I'll tell you what I'd
really like to do. Let's get out of the tub before we
turn into prunes." With a laugh, surrounding Liza
with an endearing hug, Nadine kissed her on her
cheek.

Liza turned slightly, allowing her lips to meet
Nadine's once again. "I feel so close to you .." she
said between the kisses.

"As I do to you," Nadine replied warmly. "Now up! Up! To the fire, my little prune."

Nadine rose, leaning over to a towel draped over the wooden stand. Briskly she ran the towel over Liza's body, admiring her shapely body, then wrapped her in the big fluffy towel.

"Now off with you! To the fire. I'll be right there."

Liza stepped out of the tub and then turned to Nadine, placing a soft kiss on her cheek. "I love you," she said shyly, and hurried out to the fire.

Blanketing herself in a towel, Nadine walked over to the mirror. Staring at her reflection, she smiled, rather pleased with herself. Of course it had been a *most* difficult decision, she thought as she opened a small bottle of perfume and dabbed it between her breasts. One that she had not taken lightly. She fluffed her hair just a bit. From now on she would be Liza's Miss Lavender. A new identity, yes, but in time one she felt she could become quite comfortable with. After all, look how well she had done so far! She gave her hair one last tousle and smiled slyly, thinking of Liza who was awaiting her out by the fire. Yes, Miss Lavender would take care of everything!

LILITH

They had been exploring New Orleans the entire day and as dusk began to blanket this humid city, they finally reached their destination, the French Quarter.

This was the first trip Francine and Kay had taken together and, as both had agreed over lunch, New Orleans was the perfect choice. Francine had originally pushed for New York City — for the plays, the lights, the shopping — but Kay, who was more prone to get her way most of the time anyway, had done an intense amount of research on the city of

New Orleans. After presenting a pile of pamphlets to Francine, Kay had gone on to describe the remarkable flavor of this city — the tours of the majestic old plantations full of histories and memories, the ride down the Mississippi on the Delta Queen, the musicians and tap dancers on street corners, the spicy and mysterious Cajun people. There were rumors of dark women who could read the future, hints of voodoo and of shadows that walked the night — and of course, the shopping, the restaurants, the clubs. Nevertheless, New Orleans was turning out to be even more than either of them had anticipated.

Climbing out of the back of a rather beat-up taxi, Francine handed the old black driver a ten-dollar bill. Kay, right behind her, carried the two shopping bags.

"Good evening, ladies," the wrinkled old man said with a wry smile on his face. "Keep your eyes open for Mis' Mattie. She'd be showing you the real New Orleans." He tipped his frayed straw hat and pulled the taxi away from the curb, leaving Francine and Kay deep in the heart of the French Quarter.

The sun had set, and yet the city still was hot, demanding in its heat, not even a slight breeze to offer relief from the humidity. Wiping a small bead of sweat from her brow, Kay turned to Francine and said in a curious tone, "Who do you think this Miss Mattie is?"

Francine, turning to look up and down the deserted street where the driver had left them, said quickly, "I don't know, but I have a weird feeling this isn't Bourbon Street. I did tell him Bourbon, didn't I? Where are we anyway? Damn!"

For some inexplicable reason, Francine had felt a little on edge since they had gotten out of the taxi.

Distracted by this feeling, she had let the cab driver leave without paying much attention to where they were. She walked over to the street sigh. Burton Street.

"Shit!" Francine complained. "He let us off at Burton Street. Not Bourbon."

"Oh, well," Kay answered with her usual optimistic perspective on things. "Bourbon Street can't be far. The French Quarter's not that big, is it? Let's walk up to the first main street that we reach and ask directions, or catch a cab there. No big deal."

"Okay," Francine responded, still feeling a little uneasy.

Where in the hell are we, she thought, glancing down the dark street. Up at the far end was a light, perhaps a small market, beckoning to them.

"Let's walk up to that store and get directions from there."

As they began their journey up the dark empty street, Francine couldn't help but think about the article she had read describing the hidden city of New Orleans — the one that most visitors don't see: the weaving of mysteries; voodoo; the eyes that watch from darkened alleys; the shadowless entities that allegedly call New Orleans their home.

Only their footsteps echoed — heels against concrete, click-clack . . . Around another corner, the light closer, a small sign below a welcoming halo read, "Miss Mattie Tarot Card Readings."

"Look!" Kay said excitedly. "This is what the cab driver was telling us about. Let's go in! Wouldn't it be fun!"

"I don't know . . ." Francine hesitated.

"Oh, come on!" Kay insisted, pulling Francine by

the hand up to the door. A large brass lion's head served as the knocker. Kay lifted the ring in the lion's mouth, rapping several times on the old wooden door.

Within seconds, the door opened. An old dark woman — hair hidden under a deep blue bandana, shawl wrapped around her thin frame — stood before them.

"Reading?" she questioned, staring directly into Francine's eyes. Not blinking, not smiling, just staring, as if she had been waiting for Francine.

The door creaked as it opened. Miss Mattie led the women into a small candle-lit room.

"You first," Francine whispered, nudging her friend in front of her.

Kay, sensing Francine's reluctance, walked over to the tapestry-covered table and sat directly across from where Miss Mattie had seated herself.

"Twenty," Miss Mattie said. "Two readings, twenty dollars."

Francine reached into her pocket, pulled out two tens, and placed the bills in Miss Mattie's dark palm.

"Now," Miss Mattie said, directing her gaze to Kay after quickly pushing the money into a small leather pouch. She removed a small black and gold scarf from the table to reveal a tattered deck of Tarot cards. She turned one, then two, then three cards onto the table.

"Lucky in love, aren't you?" she said in a deep monotone. "But she walks away only to return an altered woman." And with that Miss Mattie picked the cards up from the table.

"Does that mean that my relationship will —"

"Lucky in love," Miss Mattie interrupted sternly.

"But she walks away only to return an altered woman!" Quickly Miss Mattie reached over to a basket and handed Kay a small brown and black bead on a leather cord. "Wear this. Please. You must not look her in the eyes when she returns. You must send her away."

Kay opened her hand, allowing Miss Mattie to drop the necklace into her palm.

Miss Mattie looked over at Francine. "Next," she said, once again staring feverently into Francine's eyes.

Francine walked over to the table and sat down. Miss Mattie began to shuffle the cards, carefully, not turning her deep dark eyes from Francine. She flipped over one, two, three, four, five cards.

"She watches you. The mistress of the night. The labyrinth awaits you. Let this be a warning. You must leave New Orleans at once!"

Miss Mattie broke her stare and hurriedly picked up the five cards.

"I —" Francine began to ask.

"At once!" Miss Mattie said even more harshly, rising from the table, leaving the room, disappearing down the darkened hallway.

Francine, quite stunned, turned to Kay. "Well, what the hell do you suppose that means?"

"Oh, Francine," Kay said, trying to let the whole incident be more of a fun experiment than anything else. "Don't take things so seriously. That's what these people are supposed to do for the tourist. You know — mystery, voodoo . . . Come on, let's go find Bourbon Street."

With Miss Mattie not returning, Kay and Francine let themselves out. And there, in front of Miss

Mattie's brick house, sat the old man in the beat-up taxi.

"Mis' Mattie said you might be needing a ride," he said wearily, shaking his head. "That woman, she keeps me a-comin' an' a-goin'."

"Bourbon Street, please," Kay said cheerfully, trying to pull Francine out of her sudden silence and into the taxi. They climbed back into the cab and within minutes were on Bourbon Street, an extreme contrast to the dark streets they had just left. Bourbon street was alive — full of music, lights, people, saloons.

Let it go, Francine thought, as she tried to rid herself of a shadowy after-chill. *Leave New Orleans at once!* What foolishness! The heartbeat of Bourbon Street was beginning to lift the chill, to warm her. She felt light again, free of that earlier darkness.

And once again, Kay and Francine began to explore the city: in and out of clubs, dancing, drinking, listening to saxophones, jazz. Another club, another drink — they were dizzy, lightheaded. They spent the evening laughing, joking, flirting and talking at tables for two, at bars. Finally, they ended up in the quiet lounge off the lobby of the hotel they were staying in, ten minutes from the French Quarter.

They were sitting at a small table in the almost empty cocktail lounge. Francine, slightly intoxicated, leaning back against a mirrored wall slowly scanned the room: the piano player in the corner playing a sultry tune; the dim lighting — a candle in a red glass holder on each table; the bartender engrossed in conversation with a large-bosomed woman in a tight, red-sequined dress; a man and woman at another

71

table, his arms around her, leaning into each other, kissing slowly, erotically. As Francine's focus began to drift back towards Kay, she happened to notice a woman, alone, a few tables away, just sitting, looking directly at Francine.

Francine tried to look away, to see past the other tables back to lovely Kay. But no, it was as if her eyes had their own will . . . and they were choosing to stay fixed on the image of the auburn-haired woman.

She was rather striking — that glossy hair pulled away from her face into some sort of a twist. Francine couldn't see much of the woman's face, hidden as it was beneath a mesh net draped from a black velvet hat. A small gem — a diamond? — seemed to hold the net to the hat. The woman's black silk dress plunged rather low, exposing cream-colored skin, strong shoulders, the ample cleavage of her voluptuous breasts. A thin string of pearls was clasped tightly against her marvelous long neck. Francine felt hypnotized.

It was almost as if the woman had been waiting — waiting for Francine's eyes to finally find her — patiently sitting alone, sipping her drink and waiting for that very moment. And although Francine could vaguely see her eyes through the net, it seemed as if they were imploring Francine to meet her gaze. Francine felt somewhat dizzy. She could hear a faint humming somewhere, perhaps in the very heart of her soul. A tingling, a warmth, an excitement overcame her. Without turning away, the woman carefully lifted the veil — exposing first the full lips, then the chiseled nose, and finally, those burning, deep eyes. Bringing her drink to her lips — almost in a toast — she took a sip and then placed the glass back on the table.

"Francine? Francine! What in heaven's name are you staring at?" Kay demanded, turning to see exactly what Francine was so taken with.

Kay scanned the room quickly — the musician still at the piano, the bartender still in conversation with the woman in red, the man and woman, still embracing.

"Francine, I think you're drunk. Let's go up to the room, honey. You're in a stupor."

"No, please," Francine said distractedly. "You go ahead. I just think I need to relax. Be alone for a while."

"Well, I don't know what your problem is. Fine! You sit there by yourself! I'm going up to the room!"

Kay got up, looked around the bar one more time trying to see what could have mesmerized Francine. But there was nothing. Probably too much alcohol, Kay mused. Fine. Let her see what it was like to be alone!

Kay, annoyed, left the lounge, leaving Francine by herself, still entranced.

Only seconds after Kay left, the woman in black rose from the table. Graceful and fluid, as if she rode the very air itself, she walked, rather floated, over to Francine's table.

Francine could barely breathe, so taken was she by this raven-like enchantress who approached, the air around her fragrant with an exotic scent. Her eyes were green, like the forest, piercing, aware. Her cheekbones high, regal, highlighted a face even more extraordinary than Francine had anticipated.

As she reached the table, to the very place where

Kay had been sitting just moments before, she placed her smooth long fingers on the back of Francine's hand. Francine glanced down to the table, to her hand, to the long fingers. A large ruby in an antique setting adorned the middle finger of this remarkable hand. The deep fire of the stone was almost as spellbinding as the woman's jade green eyes.

"Francine," the woman said softly, her voice soothing, almost magical. "I have been waiting for you." She shifted her fingers ever so slightly, the light from the candle catching in the ruby's facets — sending a glint of red sparkle into Francine's eyes.

"But I . . ." Francine tried to respond, trying so hard to pull her eyes away from the ruby ring, yet unable to do so.

"But you do, my lovely Francine. You know me, in your soul you do. Yes. You may look at me now."

Francine felt a sudden jerk, almost as if her focus had been forced to that ruby and now it was released. Slowly, she lifted her face toward the woman. Eyes meeting eyes.

Francine felt an overwhelming rush of heat throughout her body as she stared, then fell into the woman's gaze. Once again that silent humming began — only now the sound was curiously in time with her heartbeat, in time with the blood that was pushing, surging, rushing through her now stimulated body.

"I am Lilith. How very forward of me, how very rude, approaching you without so, without so much as even a name. I want to show you the rest of New Orleans. The part you haven't seen yet . . . the hidden New Orleans."

Francine listened to the rhythmical sound of

Lilith's voice. She had an accent of some sort, unrecognizable yet so seductive and engaging.

"Yes. The hidden city," Francine heard herself saying. Those words seemed familiar — but from where, she could not say. she felt herself rising, her hand still in Lilith's almost as if they had always been connected in this way.

"Perhaps I should . . ." Francine couldn't seem to remember exactly what it was she should be doing. Something about this place . . . Was there someone waiting for her somewhere? Upstairs? She could feel an odd sensation of someone thinking, calling, crying. An image of a woman on a bed, face in her hands, weeping; she had short brown hair, lovely small breasts. She was wondering, awaiting her arrival. The image turned into small light particles that swirled and twisted like tiny fireworks and then disappeared. It was too difficult to remember.

Lilith was leading her out of the lounge, through the lobby, to the elevator. And slowly up and up in the small elevator car, they climbed to the center of the tall building. Francine huddled in the corner as Lilith, in front of her, leaned into her, pressing against her — speaking to her, coaxing her.

"I watched you outside Miss Mattie's today. Getting out of the taxi. Your lovely blonde hair, that air of uncertainty. Edginess. I felt you so strongly. I was in the darkness. No, of course you didn't see me, but you felt me, didn't you?"

She was whispering in Francine's ear as she spoke — that intoxicating perfume creating a haze in Francine's mind as Lilith's tongue darted quickly in and out of her ear between sentences.

"I wanted to have you then, to claim you, but

Miss Mattie can be so difficult at times — with her potions and charms — and all that. Tell me she wasn't." Still she whispered, circling that hot tongue around the outside of Francine's ear, down her cheek, down her neck.

Suddenly, the elevator car stopped and the doors opened wide. Francine had no idea which floor they were on. She could see the last number lit up above the elevator door. They must be many levels up from the lobby.

Lilith clasped Francine's hand and glided down the hall to a door. Again, numbers — Francine's brain was having trouble registering what the symbols on the door actually meant.

Lilith unlocked the door with a touch of that ruby-laden finger and moved lightly into the shadowy room. Francine, behind her, seemed to float along with her. Somehow the door closed. Somehow she heard it lock — once, maybe twice. The room danced in the flicker of candlelight. The scent of that unusual perfume was overwhelming in the room. Francine felt dizzy again.

A hurricane of images began twirling in her mind: the smile on the cab driver's face; Miss Mattie's strong, insistent gaze. *Let this be a warning*, Miss Mattie seemed to be saying over and over as she pointed at Francine. Kay, her palm open, held something in her hand. The bead — the thought of it stung in Francine's mind. The idea of the bead hurt. The images revolved, twisting. *Let this be a warning. Let this be a warning!*

"Enough, Francine," Lilith was saying rather firmly. "Let it go. That's a dream. Let it go." Francine looked up to Lilith who was now a few feet away, surrounded by a halo of candlelight. She was moving, provocatively in some sort of dance. Francine was again mesmerized. The storm of images evaporated. All that mattered was Lilith — lovely, lovely Lilith — pulling the silk straps from her shoulders, removing the black velvet hat, stepping out of the high black shoes, letting the dress float to the floor.

Francine felt overcome with desire. Lilith, undressed, was so exciting, her body so erotic — the shoulders strong, the breasts round and ripe with small pert nipples pointing slightly towards the ceiling. Her slim waist budding into full petal-like hips. Between her firm, full thighs, the triangular patch of dark red hair covering her secret.

Francine felt a surge of electricity shudder through her. Every part of her was alive. Her own nipples felt as though someone was rolling them, squeezing them. Her clitoris began to throb.

"Francine," Lilith murmured, a narcotic summoning the broken-down addict. "Come to me. Please. Come to me."

Francine felt compelled to walk over to Lilith. She drew Francine into her arms, circling her in a fog of intense sexuality.

"You. You are so lovely," Lilith was saying breathlessly. "I must have you." Circling, including Francine in her movement, she stopped to lift Francine's blouse, to remove Francine's pants. She stepped away from her to enjoy the beauty of Francine's body, then pulled her back in. Arms wrapped around her, Lilith's full breasts pushed into Francine's small, soft breasts. Rocking, swaying, Lilith kissed every inch of Francine's face and neck — little kisses, hot kisses, then her tongue, just her tongue licking over and over. Every bit of Francine's neck was damp with Lilith's saliva.

Lilith moved Francine onto the bed, then pulled herself down on top of Francine. Still licking, she lightly nipped her neck, shoulders, breasts.

Francine had never felt anything so overpowering. With just kisses, little bites, she was beside herself in pleasure.

Lilith propped herself directly above Francine, her face perhaps ten inches away. She was saying something, but Francine had trouble hearing or understanding the words. She looked into Lilith's face — searching for her lips, hoping somehow to see the words as they fell out of Lilith's mouth.

There was something about "forever," "everlasting," "deathless." Lilith's skin looked surprisingly pale in this light. The whites of her eyes were almost blue. What was she saying? What did she mean?'

"And it will feel so sweet. So very sweet. Letting go is the secret. Giving it up to me is the deepest pleasure of all . . ."

Lilith was pulling on Francine's large square nipples, still whispering over and over. The words, like the numbers on the door, were not making much sense.

"You are such a jewel. Such a beauty. When you first arrived in New Orleans, I could feel your presence. I have been waiting, forever it seems, for you to come to me." Lilith's words were so soft as they passed from her full lips into Francine's small available ear.

Still unable to interpret, exactly, the words — the

meaning behind Lilith's murmuring — she was able to hear the rhythm, the musical cadence of Lilith's voice — suggesting, enticing, luring Francine into a deeper trance.

"And when you finally returned to the hotel, I was beyond myself in desire for you. Seeing you across the room — talking, laughing. Hearing the intake of air as you'd inhale, feeling the warm breath of you as you exhaled. But of course, you do not realize how finely honed are my senses of sound, touch, sight. You could be miles away from me and I could smell your scent, feel your presence."

Francine's thought process no longer seemed to be functioning properly. She could barely hear at all, yet she could feel what Lilith was thinking. Francine's body, quite heavy, tingling as if asleep, was on the bed as if weighted down and yet at the very same moment it felt light, almost floating.

But the kisses, Lilith's tiny electric kisses on Francine's neck were starting to sting a little. Lilith continued to dart her tongue back and forth across a small area on Francine's soft peach-like neck while her fingers gently squeezed Francine's nipples. She pushed her firm belly down on Francine's.

Francine felt hot, very hot. Those little kisses hurt as if a snake were striking at her neck. Slashing, attempting to sear, to puncture, to poison, her tongue lashed back and forth.

"You want me, my love, don't you?" Lilith said. Still propelling her tongue, she moved her fingers between the blonde curls that protected Francine's delicate sex.

Francine could feel Lilith's finger between her swollen lips; it slid up the side of her clitoris, across

79

the shaft and down the other side. She was slippery, slick. Lilith's repeated touch was light, yet very direct. Francine felt herself arch ever so slightly to encourage Lilith's finger to press even a little harder.

Lilith, her lips flush against Francine's neck, her tongue flicking quickly, could sense Francine's readiness for more. Immediately Lilith's fingers began to search for the hard jewel between Francine's lips, and as hot as Francine was, Lilith had no difficulty finding it. Within seconds, Lilith had her at her peak — moaning, writhing in pleasure, wildly jerking in a frenzy. Lilith still rubbing her, still licking, nipping at her neck.

As Francine reached the height of her climax, Lilith let her sharp teeth pierce the soft skin on Francine's neck. In her pleasure, Francine did not immediately realize what was happening, but suddenly, the fiery ache in her neck drew her out of orgasm.

She began to struggle, to push violently at Lilith. The pain was becoming excruciating, unbearable. Lilith overpowered her with brute strength. Pinning her to the bed, she forced Francine's head to the side and clamped her lips to Francine's neck. She sucked lightly at first and then feverishly while she jerked her own clitoris up against Francine's hipbone.

Rocking back and forth, she felt the pleasure in her own clitoris as she continued to drink from Francine.

The fire began to spread throughout Francine's body — burning, searing, raging. Every part of her ignited in scalding relentless pain. And yet something was beginning to change. Along with the pain, an intense feeling of bliss, of gratification, of surrender began to emerge.

Her mind was starting to let go of the pain — starting to embrace oneness with Lilith. Lilith, still sucking, was moaning and purring, almost growling. Her body was hot; the sweat sizzled on her skin. Grasping Francine harder and harder, she jerked her mouth away and let out a guttural scream.

Francine — dazed and tense from pushing and gripping Lilith — looked up. Lilith was looking straight ahead, her eyes rolled back in their sockets. Dark blood was smeared around her full lips, her chin, her cheeks.

"Mine!" she screeched in fury. *"Mine!"*

Kay was startled by the light scraping on her hotel room door. A chill ran through her tired body. She had been waiting hours for Francine's return — alternating between crying, pacing, calling the lobby, the lounge — swearing angrily, praying desperately. She was exhausted, depleted.

"Francine?" Kay whispered as she turned toward the door.

Nothing.

"Francine?" Kay asked, raising her voice. "Is that you?"

Kay placed her ear against the cool wooden door frame. "Is that you?" she repeated, feeling a sudden sense of vulnerability.

You must send her away. You must send her away. Miss Mattie's words suddenly came into her mind.

"Francine?"

"Yes," Francine responded.

"Yes, dear Kay, please let me in."

Kay quickly unlocked the door and pulled it open. Without warning, Kay was stunned by the striking scent of oranges and anise that seemed to surround Francine. Kay felt faint, dazed. She stepped back, shaking her head, as if trying to force away this sudden lightheadedness.

Dizzy, she attempted to center herself, trying to focus on Francine who, in the dim light, looked pale and worn, almost limp. Kay opened her eyes wider, as if trying to let more light in, to see more clearly. Dark circles were under Francine's once-vibrant blue eyes. There was a certain vacantness to her gaze. Kay looked slowly from Francine's face down to her bruised, swollen neck.

"What in God's name?" Kay cried out, pulling Francine into the room.

"I came to take you with me," Francine whispered as she staggered into the room, her eyes glazed. The energy she emitted was a mixture of hot and cold, light and dark.

"What are you talking about?" Kay demanded, forcing herself to look at the floor, for some reason not wanting to meet Francine's eyes.

"You must come with me. I've seen the hidden city of New Orleans, dear Kay. It awaits you . . . us." Francine seemed more on edge now, a little frantic. As she grasped Kay's hand, she pleaded,

"Come. Come with me. To a place where it is so warm and so . . ."

Kay was enticed by that unusual fragrance Francine was wearing. Unable to make sense of things, she tried to step back, to appraise. Slowly, she allowed her eyes to drift back up toward Francine's neck. The bruise, deep purple in color was framed by two small tears in the slightly swollen flesh. A silver chain brushed the bruised area. Kay's eyes followed the necklace to an antique ruby pendant that rested right in the hollow of Francine's neck. The light from the room seemed to hit the stone's facets just so, sending a glimmer of red fire from the ruby into Kay's eye. The effect was compelling. It was difficult to turn away from that entrancing sparkle.

Suddenly, Francine's grip became stronger, more forceful. She was forcing Kay into her arms, grabbing her, pinning her against the wall — kissing, nipping, almost biting her neck.

Francine's sudden shift from frailness to intense strength took Kay by surprise. She was stunned, taken off guard.

Francine was struggling, forcing Kay's head to the side, trying to bite into Kay's vulnerable neck. Suddenly Kay had a clear understanding — beautiful, wonderful Francine was no longer Francine at all.

"No!" she screamed, panicked. "No! Francine, no. No!" She was punching, kicking, flailing her arms — anything to push Francine away. She fought with all her strength.

Kay ran to the bed and grabbed a pillow, a hanger, a paperback book — as if any of these things could protect her. Could stop Francine!

She backed into a corner, between the bed and the bureau, and at that moment, arms full of useless weapons, she remembered the bead on the leather necklace. Words began to twirl in her mind: *Send her away. Do not look her in the eye!* She dropped the hanger, book and pillow and grabbed the necklace, quickly putting it over her head.

"Look at me, Kay. Please." Francine said softly, her voice suddenly filled with the love and compassion it used to have.

Kay, still in the corner, lifted the bead between her thumb and forefinger. She was confused. She knew that she absolutely must send Francine away immediately! And yet, she could not help but remember the depth of the love they had shared. She wanted so much to look, one last time, into her lover's eyes — to connect, just once more, before sending her away forever.

Francine, as if sensing Kay's thoughts, slowly moved across the room. Tenderly, she reached out her long pale fingers and gently cupped Kay's face. Using the subtlest pressure, she began to lift Kay's chin.

Eyes to meet eyes, Francine thought, hungrily summoning all the power within her to appear loving. *Just one look and she's mine.*

ROBERTA

"What a night!" Roberta burst into the room where her roommate Jeanette was lazily lounging on the bed.

"Did you meet her?" Jeanette responded with interest, pushing herself up from the pillows into a sitting position. "Was she there? Did you tell her?"

"Let me get my shoes off," Roberta replied, pulling her black silver-heeled boots from her tired feet. She fell onto the bed next to Jeanette and hugged her.

"I wasn't sure if she'd be there. I mean, Marilyn

85

said she goes to that meeting on Friday nights . . . but she wasn't there last week and so I wasn't sure she'd be there tonight. But you know me," Roberta smiled, full of spirit, giving Jeanette's hair a quick tousle. "I've been bored lately. And I swear, Jeanette, this woman Cynthia is so hot. You know how picky I am. I never see anyone who interests me. But when I first saw her at Marilyn's party, I couldn't get her out of my mind. Calling around trying to find out who she was, where she worked . . ."

"Yeah," Jeanette teased, "and not letting the fact that she's in a relationship stop you."

"Okay, okay! I don't want to marry the woman! I just wanted to, well, spend a little time — okay, so I wanted her to know I was taken with her, that's all. I couldn't help it. I never see women I like. You know that — no one will ever take Mandy's place. And now that she's gone from my life once and for all, if the rare occasion occurs where I see someone who turns me on, I guess I feel like I need to pursue it."

"Go on, go on!" Jeanette said with a laugh. "You already rationalized this whole thing to me when you first decided to tell Cynthia you had a crush on her. So get on with it — what happened tonight?"

"Well, I got to the place where the meeting was being held." Roberta paused, trying to create an air of anticipation. "And there it was, the blue truck she drives, right next to Marilyn's. The meeting was still in progress, so I walked over and kind of peeked into the driver's side. Nothing much really — a notebook, sunglasses. I still wasn't quite sure how I was actually going to approach her. I knew I had about ten more minutes till the meeting let out. It was

86

getting kind of dark, so I walked into the field directly behind where the truck was parked and sat there — just to evaluate my plan of attack and to watch for her to come out of the building."

"Oh, Roberta, you're too much!" Jeanette jumped up. "Let me get some juice; I'll be right back."

Roberta, lying back onto the bed, closed her eyes and dreamily let her mind wander.

Cynthia had been driving almost half an hour. It was already an hour and a half later than the time she had told Davern to expect her home. The forty-five-minute drive up to the cabin didn't help things. What in God's name would she tell Davern? Definitely not the truth — things were going well between them . . . This thing with the woman in black was just that — a thing. How often did an opportunity like that come along? It was a surprise. No time to use judgement, that's for sure!

Still swimming in the images from that earlier encounter, Cynthia almost missed the turn-off onto the curvy mountain road that led up to the cabin. Quickly, she veered the truck to the right and headed up the hill.

She had walked out of the meeting — actually she was one of the last ones to leave — crossed the street and unlocked her truck. Just as she had climbed in and closed the door, the most incredibly erotic woman had stepped out of the darkness and walked directly over toward the truck.

She was wearing black boots, a black miniskirt,

and a black leather jacket. A bouquet of curls surrounded her sensuous face, dark, burning eyes, full, painted lips.

She reached the truck and lightly tapped on the window.

Cynthia, somewhat taken aback, rolled down her window. Immediately the woman began speaking, her voice almost a murmur — purring would be a better way to describe it.

Cynthia, still trying to concentrate on the windy road, was once again mesmerized by the memory of the woman's eyes, her scent, the deep suggestiveness of her voice.

"I need to speak with you," the woman had said alluringly, with some sort of mysterious vagueness to her tone.

"Sure," Cynthia replied.

"Perhaps we could walk a bit?" The woman stepped back.

Cynthia opened the door and walked over toward the woman. Cynthia was taller. Standing next to her, Cynthia realized that this woman would probably fit into her arms perfectly. Where this thought came from, Cynthia could not imagine. She was very much in love with Davern. They had been together for four years and not once had Cynthia ever looked at another woman, let alone thought about . . .

Cynthia, still somewhat dazed, pulled the truck over to the side of the road. There was no way she could go home just yet. She needed to think, to sort things out.

Turning off the motor, she leaned back in the seat and closed her eyes. Again she was able to visualize the woman stepping out of the darkness, her small curved body framed in a glow of light from the street lamp, her red hair and brown eyes all aflame.

The tapping on the window, the woman's scent as she approached Cynthia, that sultry voice . . .

She and the woman had begun to walk. The woman kept repeating herself, saying that she needed to talk, if she could, for just a minute, if perhaps Cynthia wouldn't mind.

Cynthia followed her into the darkness. The further she moved from her truck, the deeper she walked into the unknown, the more the coolness of the night air seemed to warm.

Then the woman abruptly stopped to turn and face Cynthia. "I saw you at the party," she said breathlessly. "I was so taken by your looks, your style . . . I started asking questions — this friend, that friend — until I tracked you down to this meeting."

There was a sort of husky desperation to the woman's voice, as though she needed something from Cynthia, now, and that no one else could help her.

Still deep in thought, Cynthia let out a deep sigh, rolling her truck window down slightly to let the coolness of the air in. She glanced at her watch; she was almost two hours late. She should start the truck, head home to Davern. Cynthia closed her eyes and floated back to the field, back to that woman.

"I know, I mean, I heard that you were in a relationship — and I'm not really sure of the appropriateness of this — but all I want is tonight.

89

Just tonight. In the darkness. You and I. Who's to know?"

"I'm very married," Cynthia replied, trying to keep a tone of conviction in her voice — but the words seemed so light, so frivolous.

"Yes. You are. And that's why, after tonight, we never have to meet again. But now, for this moment, we're in a pocket of the night. It's like we've stepped out of our other lives for just this one time. No one's to know. Just you and I."

She reached up to Cynthia and kissed her in such a way that Cynthia felt her legs weaken. Within seconds, she had allowed herself to fall into this woman's arms and together they capsized onto the roughness of the ground.

Rolling in her arms, she tumbled over and over as the woman slid her soft, hot tongue in and out of Cynthia's yielding mouth. The woman, now moaning deeply, unexpectedly stopped rolling and quickly mounted Cynthia. She pushed her night-cooled hands up Cynthia's blouse and rubbed her hands roughly across her firm breasts.

"You can't imagine," the woman said feverishly, "how much I've wanted you. How I've fantasized about this very moment."

She continued to run her hands over Cynthia's breasts as she leaned down and began kissing Cynthia again — first the lips, then her face and finally her vulnerable neck — her tongue cool from speaking, from having entered the night air.

Cynthia began to feel sucked into the darkness. She tried to look over to where her truck was parked near the street lamp, but she felt totally enveloped in the night . . . a different world. Perhaps this woman was right. Just the two of them. Who's to know?

The woman straddling her — taking off her jacket, then lifting off that pink blouse — was beautiful and alluring. Cynthia lay in awe, her back against the coarse grass, watching her remove the pink lace bra. Two very soft breasts appeared with the rosiest nipples Cynthia had ever seen.

Cynthia, feeling herself drift into the safety of the night, gently cupped the woman's smooth breast. "What a beauty," she whispered, beginning to pull on the thimble-shaped nipple, which hardened in immediate response to Cynthia's attentions, as if it were begging for more.

"Oh!" the woman exclaimed. "Your touch arouses me so . . . Please —" She took Cynthia's other hand and directed it up her skirt. "I'm not wearing any panties."

Cynthia was overwhelmed by the tantalizing scent that suddenly surrounded her as the woman squatted over her. Without warning, a beam of light hit Cynthia in the eyes.

"Oh, so sorry," the woman said, quickly angling a small flashlight away from Cynthia's face and turning it so the light was directed up her black skirt.

"Can you see?" the woman whispered, ignoring the question. "Can you see how hot I am? I'm swollen, aren't I? Just from kissing you. Please. Put your fingers into me. I want you to see just how aroused I am."

Cynthia could not bear it any longer. This woman had the most perfect pussy: small, defined lips lightly covered in auburn curls; that tongue of a clitoris sticking out from the lips too small to contain the whole wedge of flesh; those smaller, butterfly-like lips that glistened with moisture. Without hesitation Cynthia forced two of her fingers into the heat of the woman's tight slit. Forcing them further, even further into the warmth, she increased the motion as she began to fuck her rapidly. The woman rode Cynthia's fingers, bouncing faster and faster. The woman's fragrance was even more intoxicating. Cynthia's whole hand was wet and sticky.

Expertly, Cynthia slipped another finger into her as the woman's pace continued. The flashlight had dropped to the ground but was angled in such a way that Cynthia could watch this steaming pussy sucking up and down on her three, now four fingers.

Cynthia began to lose control, as though she were stepping over some imaginary boundary onto a wilder side. She felt herself desiring more, wanting to risk it all, to go further than she'd ever been.

The woman was so slippery, so open. Cynthia, not caring about anything else, permitted her hand to close into a fist and within seconds the woman had taken Cynthia's whole fist up into her vagina.

The woman let out a guttural, primitive sound as she moved vigorously up and down, over and over — taking one of her own fingers and lashing it wildly back and forth across her distended clitoris.

Cynthia was swept into a whirlwind of passion. The sight of this woman uncontrollably fucking her hand as she simultaneously slapped her own clit back and forth directly in front of Cynthia's face was too much for her. She felt her own body involuntarily arching with desire.

At that very moment, the woman's whole body tightened around Cynthia's hand as she let out a low, deep groan. "Oh my God. Oh my God. Oh my God," she cried out in ecstasy. Slowly she lifted off of Cynthia's hand and collapsed into Cynthia's arms, her entire body damp with perspiration. She sighed, her body relaxed. "You," she whispered in Cynthia's ear. "You. You. You."

Rekindled, the woman began to unbutton Cynthia's jeans and pull them off. "I want to feel you. That's what I want. From that first moment that I saw you I tried to imagine your scent. Your warmth. Oh yes," she said, her voice sizzling as she slipped her hands between Cynthia's legs, down into Cynthia's own moist well of desire.

Quickly, she lifted her fingers from Cynthia's wetness to her own lips, spreading the moisture around her mouth and slowly letting her tongue lick the dew.

She reached for the small flashlight, knelt between Cynthia's legs, and watched her fingers explore every little crevice of Cynthia's throbbing pussy.

"I'm on fire!" Cynthia's voice was almost pleading. She felt her lips being pulled apart. "I'm *so* hot. Please!"

"Yes, Cynthia. Yes," the woman said calmly. "I know just what you want. Sit up a bit. I want you to watch this."

Cynthia propped herself on her elbows as the woman, still aiming the flashlight at Cynthia's full lips, began to pull her wide apart.

"Over the edge, that's when it's erotic. Just taking it a step further, don't you agree?" The intonation sharpened. "Like you fisting me, or like me doing this to you."

And with that she pushed the lit end of the small flashlight into Cynthia's pounding pussy.

Quickly she pulled it out just enough to allow the light to send a glow around Cynthia's red pussy, and then inserted it again. Still spreading her, the woman continued moving the flashlight in and drawing it out to light up those thick, flushed lips.

"Lean up and touch yourself," the woman demanded.

Cynthia leaned forward and was afforded an excellent view of the mushroom-shaped head of the flashlight squeezing in and then being dragged out, lighting up her pussy with each outward stroke. The flashlight so smooth, its small bulb so warm.

She licked her own finger, covering it with saliva and then slid it directly to the special spot she always touched when she masturbated. Slowly at first, she nudged her thickened shaft, mesmerized by the erratic burst of light, as the woman thrust the flashlight in and out.

Recklessly, Cynthia began to increase the motion of her fingers, prodding her clit in rhythm with the ribbed flashlight — first the darkness, then the flash of light. She now slapped and thumped her clitoris with her whole hand, watching the light flash faster, faster until Cynthia exploded into orgasm, lunging deeper and deeper onto the flashlight. She grabbed the woman's mane of curls and screamed with pleasure.

"That's right. That's right," the woman kept repeating. "You and me. You and me."

Cynthia was floating — her cunt throbbed as the woman pulled the flashlight out and up toward her face.

"Take a good look at me," she said confidently. "So when you want to track me down you'll be able to describe what you're looking for." She laughed, grabbed the bra, her pink top and leather jacket, and then disappeared into the darkness.

Cynthia turned on the interior light of her truck, trying to bring herself back from the vision of that woman, the bewitchment that she now felt. Still entranced, she flicked off the light, started up her truck and resumed the trip home.

"So anyway," Roberta said as Jeanette walked back into the room, a large glass of juice in her hand. "When she came out of the meeting, I did just what you said to do. I walked up to her, just as she was getting into her truck. I tried to be, you know, classy. Not like I was coming on to her — I let her know that I had sort of a crush on her and that if she and her girlfriend ever broke up — to look me up. Then I walked away."

"That's it? Didn't you at least tell her your name?" Jeanette asked, evidently baffled.

"Well, I figure, if she really wants to find me, she will. I think I left a lasting impression."

MORRIGAN

Jennifer looked down the long aisle. Row upon
row of cereal boxes seemed to stare back at her.
White boxes, red boxes. Natural, sugar-coated.
Family-sized, single serving. It was Monday, late
afternoon, her usual shopping day. She paused, then
slowly began to push the full cart down the last aisle.
She pulled a large yellow and white box off the shelf
and placed it on top of the other groceries. The cart
needed a touch of yellow. Okay, so it wasn't on her
list, but Jennifer was tired of the same old thing.

Today she'd take a risk, try something new . . . the yellow box for sure.

With that, her last item, she sped to the checkout line. Each counter had a line of people. She chose the shortest line and picked up a magazine for something to do while she waited.

The gossip and excitement of someone else's life enticed her. Names and pictures leapt out at her.

Surveying two blue-haired ladies in the next aisle, she moved ahead to the sundries counter — M&M's and Lifesavers, razor blades, batteries. The woman in front of her wore a black lace-like tee shirt and a black suede belt. Rhinestone sunglasses were hooked through the belt.

Jennifer tried to read the next sentence in the story but her mind wouldn't focus on the words. She couldn't take her eyes off that black lace tee shirt and shiny pair of sunglasses on the woman's belt.

She was compelled by those remarkable frames — so simple, yet so entrancing. Innocent, yet suggestive.

Jennifer, quite distracted, let the magazine drop into her cart. And without really a thought, without so much as an idea of what she could possibly be considering, she heard herself say rather bluntly, "Gosh, are those prescription sunglasses?" Was there a bit of a flirtatious tone to her voice? She wasn't sure. It was so unlike her, really, to even talk to strangers, let alone a woman — well, a woman like the one in front of her.

Jennifer looked her over: the tee shirt, snug and lacy, black, skin-tight jeans, black boots with silver heel plates and thick stacked heels that emphasized her calves.

It was not like Jennifer to speak to strangers, especially someone like that woman with the rhinestone glasses.

"Want to find out?" the woman responded in a cool tone, turning towards Jennifer. Her curly dark brown hair, pulled back into a low loose pony tail, revealed a large gold hoop earring, pirate-like, in one ear.

Jennifer felt herself blush. Heat filled her entire body. The woman who stood in front of her was quite striking in her hard, tough beauty.

She pulled the sunglasses from her belt and walked past her cart over to Jennifer.

She had a scent about her — spice, Musk? Jennifer couldn't really decide, but the fragrance was, for lack of a better word, persuasive.

The woman deftly pulled off Jennifer's own thick-lensed glasses and replaced them with her electrifying rhinestone sunglasses.

"What do you think?" the woman asked in a low husky voice, simultaneously turning Jennifer toward the small mirror directly above the razor blade display. "Do you like the way you look? Exotic, quite exciting, I'd say."

Jennifer stood on tiptoes trying to see her reflection in the mirror. Visions of herself on the town — no longer "just Jennifer," no longer "just blending in," but, rather, alluring, even exotic — raced through her mind.

"You know," Jennifer said, somewhat flustered, "I can't really even see more than two inches in front of my face without my glasses . . . so I'm not quite sure how I look." She was leaning forward, holding onto her cart for support, trying to get as close to the mirror as possible, distracted by the fantasy of a new, much more provocative Jennifer.

"Sixty-four dollars and eighty five cents," the checkout girl said.

"Yes, of course," the woman answered, turning away from Jennifer, at the same time pushing Jennifer's thick glasses into the belt loop that usually housed her rhinestone sunglasses. She pulled out four twenty-dollar bills, paid, received her change, and paused to scribble something on a piece of paper.

Jennifer, still inches away from the mirror, lost in fantasy, was startled when the woman leaned close to her ear, firmly putting her hand on Jennifer's waist and pulling her close.

"I'm sure you'll be looking for me, that is, once you can see again!" she said with a laugh, lifting the rhinestone glasses from Jennifer's face, forcing a folded piece of paper into Jennifer's breast pocket, and then abruptly turning away. Within seconds she had grabbed her two bags of groceries and disappeared from the store.

Jennifer, in a daze, was not quite sure of what was going on until the checkout girl pulled her cart forward, jerking Jennifer's hand off the grocery basket, snapping her back into reality.

"Hey!" Jennifer cried out as she lost her balance, stumbling two steps forward. "Where's that woman? The one with the rhinestone glasses?" Jennifer was nervously squinting, trying to make sense of the colorful, blurred images around her.

"She left," the checkout girl said, unaware of Jennifer's dilemma.

"That woman took my glasses!" Jennifer responded, becoming more alarmed by her situation.

"Oh, come on!" The girl laughed. "This is the best thing I've seen yet!"

"No, really!" Jennifer replied anxiously. "I'm stuck here! I can't see a thing!"

"You mean you didn't know that woman?"

"No. Someone needs to run out to the parking lot and stop her!" Jennifer was almost pleading.

At this point, people were beginning to stare. Even the blue-haired ladies had put the magazine down. Something better, much better was happening at checkout counter number one. A red-haired, freckle-faced bagboy ran out into the parking lot, stopped, stood for a moment, his hand shielding his eyes from the glare of the setting sun, then re-entered the store. Trying to hold back a smile, he pressed his lips together and then said, "That lady just pulled out of the parking lot. She was driving a black Porsche . . . pretty cool, huh?"

"Jeff!" the checkout girl said crossly. "We need to help the customer. Get Mr. Lassiter. Tell him we need some sort of help here!"

Jennifer, meanwhile, felt a light layer of sweat cover her body. The fact that she was literally immobilized without her eyeglasses was a bad enough circumstance, but the embarrassment and humiliation were even worse. Everyone in the store was talking about her, pointing at Jennifer — a prisoner to her grocery cart.

How could I have ever gotten into this? she thought as the manager told the red-haired bagboy to call a taxi and the crowd watched as the manager guided her outside. He and the taxi driver loaded her groceries into the trunk.

Once home, the cab driver and Mrs. Thornton, her nosy neighbor, led her stumbling to her apartment, and finally, even as the cab driver searched her top drawer and found her spare glasses, she continued to badger herself for her brainlessness.

She was never more ashamed, never more embarrassed — the crowd of people giggling at her helplessness, while she stood there hanging onto a grocery cart for dear life!

Jennifer finished putting her groceries away, poured herself a glass of wine and fell into the over-stuffed chair in her living room. With a sigh she closed her eyes, trying to relax, to forget, but the image of that woman invaded her thoughts. She remembered that woman's enticing fragrance, those rhinestone glasses, sparkling and inviting, and felt the shock as the grocery cart was pulled from her, leaving her stumbling carelessly at the checkout counter. The fantasy of "the new Jennifer" with the sizzling glasses juxtaposed against the reality of the real Jennifer — being pointed at, the butt of a very bad joke.

And that woman's icy beauty! Her eyes, how they had looked when the woman had first faced Jennifer! Jennifer could feel them burning as they glared at her. The brazenness of that woman! To take her glasses! To humiliate her in such a way!

The more Jennifer tried to forget, the more she remembered each detail, every part of that afternoon's events, every feeling — over and over and over again.

Suddenly she realized that one very important item had slipped her mind: the note in her breast pocket. With a jerk, Jennifer lunged forward in the chair and ripped the small folded paper from her pocket, trying not to tear it in her eagerness. As she unfolded it, her body was alive with anticipation.

A chill ran through her as she glanced down at the wrinkled piece of paper. A name. Morrigan. A phone number. Smeared, barely legible. Jennifer, distressed at not being able to read the number clearly, moved closer to the lamp next to her chair. She held the paper closer to the light but the numbers were blurred, unreadable.

"Well, who cares anyway!" she said aloud. "As if I would want to call her! As if I would need this number!" Angrily, she wadded the paper and threw it across the room.

Falling back into the chair, she took a sip of wine. The alcohol was tart and she winced. She looked across the room at that small uneven ball of paper resting so innocently by the bookcase — as if it were just that, a simple ball of paper.

"I do not care!" she said again, quite sternly, staring at the paper as if it could hear, would report all it heard back to Morrigan, its mistress.

She took another sip of wine. The harshness of the day's events was beginning to dissipate. She was starting to feel the alcohol, starting to relax, to feel more herself. She closed her eyes and saw a quick image of the golden hoop, the dark hair pulled back, the silver-plated heels. Dreamy, much calmer now, she opened her eyes, just the smallest bit, just to peek. The paper was still there . . . no, of course it hadn't moved. It was harmless, not the enemy at all.

She poured another glass of wine, occasionally rechecking to make sure that the paper was still waiting. Distracted, she tried to read, pouring another glass of wine; she let herself go even further. Until finally, three or four glasses of wine later, Jennifer was quite dizzy, perhaps even drunk. She was barely able to walk; she crawled on her hands and knees across the room to the bookcase where, very carefully, she lifted the small ball of paper.

She had been at the phone for an hour, pushing every combination of numbers she could think of — writing them down, crossing them off. The wine had worn off between wrong numbers and no answers, no Morrigan. Frustrated, feeling empty and at a loss, Jennifer finally dozed off to sleep, telephone in one hand, small wrinkled paper in the other.

Over the next two weeks, Jennifer became more and more obsessed with wanting to find Morrigan. Every day after work she stopped at the grocery store — always looking down the aisles, hoping to see her, to catch the scent of her. She bought boxes of cereal, magazines, using any excuse to stop at the store, to scan the aisles.

She tried the phone numbers every day. Still no answers. No Morrigan. Each night, she tossed restlessly, only to wake in a hot sweat, aroused and disoriented.

Each day at work, she couldn't concentrate, daydreaming out the window, barely present at all. Two weeks drifted into three, then four. Jennifer, late one Thursday afternoon, a month later, passed the grocery store driving home from work, and promised herself that *this* time she would not stop. This time she would go straight home. With a quick glance she looked over to the grocery store as if to say "no more!" and at that very moment, in that brief glance, she saw it. In the parking lot, not far from the street, a black Porsche.

Jennifer swerved from the center lane to the right, almost hitting a car. Not even thinking, by rote, she turned into the parking lot and raced across the lot. She jumped out of her car, hurried over to the Porsche, and peered in the window. And there on the passenger seat were the rhinestone glasses lying on a black silken scarf.

Jennifer, heart pounding, got back into her car, and began to wait. At any moment, Morrigan would come out, would walk with that cool, confident stride toward the car, and Jennifer would . . . what? Jump out? Calmly roll down her window? Say hello?

She took a deep breath, glancing at the store entrance and back to the Porsche. Five-thirty dragged into six p.m. The red-haired bagboy came out of the store and began collecting stray carts. He noticed Jennifer, gave her a slight nod, waved. Six-thirty, the minutes crept by, seven p.m. It was dark now and still no Morrigan. Jennifer was tense, on edge — not wanting to stay, not daring to leave, to miss the chance of finally connecting with Morrigan.

Once again, the bagboy circled the lot, gathering carts one last time, looking over at Jennifer parked next to the sleek black Porsche. Did he know? Jennifer wondered, feeling embarrassed and ill at ease. Was she a joke at this store? She was there every night, walking the aisles, distracted, obsessed. Did the employees look at each other and smile knowingly, laugh behind her back?

She sank down a little in her car, as if to

104

camouflage herself, to blend in. At least her car was roomy, comfortable. She glanced back to the store, across the parking lot, over to the street. A silver Mercedes Sedan, slowly pulling up to the curb, caught Jennifer's attention. The passenger door opened, and a small flash of light exposed the occupants. Two women quickly embraced and the passenger climbed out of the car. Could it be? Jennifer sat up, alert, leaning forward, straining to see. It was Morrigan! Still spotlighted by the light from the Mercedes, she was dressed in black, hair pulled back. High, stiletto-heeled boots. She wore the same black leather jacket, full at the shoulders, cut sharply to the narrow waist. Jennifer could hear her laugh, see her slam the door, and, silhouetted in the light from the Mercedes' headlight, strut toward her Porsche, toward Jennifer. Jennifer was overcome with excitement. She could hardly breathe, her heart pounded as Morrigan approached, confident and certain.

Morrigan took her time. She was not surprised to see the woman still parked next to her Porsche. When she had first spotted her from the window inside the store (was it five? five-fifteen?) she had laughed aloud. Finally, this woman had found her! It was going to be played out as Morrigan originally planned. She had intentionally given the woman an illegible phone number that day in the grocery store, had purposely avoided this store for a month, and finally returned, parking so obviously close to the street. She really hadn't expected it to happen the *very* first day that she reappeared at the store!

Having seen that woman peering into her Porsche, Morrigan had calculated her exit through the back entrance, called a good friend, and left, making this little innocent wait two, two and a half hours in the parking lot. How easy it had been! A piece of cake really! And now, Jennifer, like a helpless fly, gently landed in a beautiful woven web; how sweetly Morrigan the patient spider would take her.

Morrigan, keeping her walk cool and deliberate, slowly approached her car, unlocked the door and slid into the driver's seat. Clicking on the interior light, she adjusted her leather jacket collar in the rear view mirror with one hand, carefully reaching for the rhinestone glasses with her other hand, covertly slipping them into her pocket, barely lifting her arm as she did so.

Suddenly, she heard a short beep from the car horn next door. she turned her head slowly. Jennifer had turned on her interior light and was staring over at Morrigan, motioning Morrigan to come over.

Morrigan gave her a nod. She did not smile — did not acknowledge Jennifer, really. Just a nod. She got out of her car and walked over to the passenger side of Jennifer's car. It was unlocked. She slid into the seat.

"Hello, again," Jennifer was saying quickly, flustered, seemingly light-headed. Morrigan gave Jennifer a look intended to pierce directly through her, to unnerve her and burn as it penetrated her.

"We won't need this," Morrigan whispered in that sultry voice, clicking off the car's interior light. The car filled with that familiar spicy scent Jennifer could not forget.

Jennifer, intoxicated by Morrigan's fragrance,

barely moved as she felt her brand new tortoise-shell glasses being lifted from her face. She briefly saw a flash of silver in the dim glow of the parking lot lights as Morrigan quickly pulled the rhinestone glasses from her pocket and placed them where Jennifer's tortoise-shell glasses had sat only moments before. In the same movement, Morrigan slipped Jennifer's glasses into the pocket of her leather jacket.

With a hot, deep sigh Morrigan opened the car door, swiftly pushed her seat back into a reclining position, and pulled Jennifer's legs across the front seat. Wasting no time, she grabbed Jennifer's right ankle, pulling her leg toward the back of the passenger's seat.

Jennifer was so taken off guard, so stunned, that she couldn't move, even if she had thought to do so.

Morrigan was whispering, muttering something under her breath as she pushed up Jennifer's skirt, as she ripped her panty hose and tore off her lace panties.

"So innocent, such a fool!" Morrigan snapped as she became aware of a single bead of sweat slowly working its way down between her breasts. She was beginning to feel her own arousal; she was wet with the anticipation of taking this rose.

"I . . ." Jennifer tried responding but was immediately silenced. Morrigan had wadded up her panties and stuffed them into her mouth.

"Not a word from you!" Morrigan said harshly. "This is what you've wanted, haven't you, little lady? Little femme girl who flirts with strangers. Flirts with danger!"

Jennifer was quiet. Although Morrigan had turned

off the car's light, there was enough light from the parking lot's tall lamps to enable Jennifer to see Morrigan leaning over her, down low. Morrigan pushed her hand up to Jennifer's crotch and pulled her left leg wider. She forced her face deep into Jennifer's sex.

Morrigan, determined in her action, began to slowly glide her tongue back and forth across Jennifer's hardening clitoris.

"So, the little lady likes it!" Morrigan gloated, lifting her head from Jennifer's succulent sugar-coated labia. She peered at Jennifer's face — eyes half-closed, mouth held open with the white lace between those pink lady-like lips.

Morrigan lifted enough to slide one, then two, and finally three fingers into Jennifer's tight, slick vagina. Roughly, she began to push her fingers deeper and then pull them rapidly out, alternating between her tongue and her fingers. Jennifer moaning — arching up in pleasure to meet each stroke.

"A mouse on the outside, but a tigress underneath!" Morrigan laughed, once again burying her face into Jennifer's spicy softness, pushing against her fleshy folds, engulfing her cheeks, chin, and nose in the delicate pinkness. Circling her face over and over in the honey-like juices, she slowly let her finger move its way into Jennifer's secret entrance further back behind her vagina.

"Is this what you like? Is this how you want it?" Morrigan whispered, her breath hot against Jennifer's soft thigh.

"I'm not sure, I've never had . . ." At that very moment, Jennifer involuntarily tensed, tried to struggle, yet paradoxically lunged forward to allow

Morrigan better access. Jennifer took a deep breath, trying to relax, suddenly enjoying the new sensations.

Morrigan's finger expertly traced a small circle against the layer of skin on the roof of Jennifer's small crevice, simultaneously inserting her thumb into Jennifer's moist vagina, gently pressing the floor of that canal. Morrigan's thumb and index finger massaged the thin layer of skin from above, from below, increasing the pressure. Jennifer, overwhelmed with sensation, began to see, feel colors exploding throughout her body. Never had she felt so good, so aroused. So hot! She blasted into orgasm, her entire body shuddering as Morrigan continued the pressure in her vagina, in her anus. The pleasure was excruciatingly delicious — unbearable, gratifying. Suddenly, almost brutally, Morrigan withdrew from Jennifer and clicked on the car light.

Jennifer, still wearing the rhinestone glasses, her skirt hiked up, stared back at Morrigan's dark blurred image.

Morrigan recited a phone number, her voice detached, with a slightly inviting undertone to it.

She took one more look at Jennifer — spread-eagled across the front seat, partially undressed, flushed from orgasm — slid out of the car, stood up, adjusted her leather jacket, and ran her fingers through her hair.

"I'm sure you'll be looking for me, that is, once you can see again!" Morrigan coolly turned, walked over to her car, got in and drove off.

SAYRE

Barbara loved the ocean, especially at times like this, when she needed to be alone, to think things through — for instance, this whole thing that had been going on the last few months. She hadn't really been ready to start dating again: the heartbreaking dissolution of her three-year relationship with Diane had pretty much cooled her down as far as getting involved with anyone again was concerned. So to fill up the vacant hours, she had decided to take a massage class at the Junior College. Perhaps it was a coincidence that she had been partnered with the only other lesbian in the class, or maybe it was fate, but one thing had just naturally led to another. And now, here she was four months later in a somewhat hot and heavy relationship with her massage partner.

It had started when Barbara mentioned a poetry reading she was going to attend after class one day. Her partner had offered to join her, which led to chats over coffee, movies on Friday evenings, and before Barbara realized how fast things had progressed, they were lovers.

Barbara looked out to the ocean and drew the collar of her jacket closer to her neck. The breeze was quite chilly today, although not at all unusual for an autumn afternoon in Northern California.

She listened as the waves called for her attention, lifting and cascading in a water show of power. It was breathtaking, with the ability to lighten the burden of any problem Barbara might have. God only knew how many hours she had spent just staring out into the sea, trying to let the saltwater stream of her tears return home to Mother Ocean. In those days after she had found Diane in bed with another woman, she had cried and screamed until the ocean would finally reach out to her with its gentle encircling breeze, embracing Barbara until all the tears had found their way home.

She wasn't quite sure if she was just being paranoid as a result of her experience with Diane, or if she should heed the insistent nagging of her intuition. Something told her that her new lover had taken another lover on the side. Sayre had been acting different lately, as though she were keeping secrets. Sayre never really opened up completely anymore, and during the last few weeks, always had some sort of tangled story about where she had been, what she'd been doing.

Barbara, spying a pearl-white shell partially buried in the damp sand, stooped down to take a closer look. Searching for pieces of the sea's jewelry, like this shell that she was now dusting off, was another reason she could spend hours on the beach. She ran her finger over the smooth edge and then placed the small treasure in her jacket pocket.

She continued her walk along the beach, eyeing the sand for another find. Perhaps she was going about things all wrong, she thought, scanning the sand. Karen and Marlene, for example, and Linda and Bettina — all of her friends had had at some time, a little fling on the side. What had Marlene said? "It's a kind of insurance . . . keeps you from feeling too vulnerable if your lover ever walks out." Like the devastating way Barbara had felt the day she found Diane with Alicia . . . and Diane talking about how she had been planning on breaking up with Barbara for quite some time, how she was *so sorry* that Barbara had found out "in such an unpleasant way."

Barbara angrily buried the tip of her boot in the sand and nudged a broken sand dollar out, kicking it a short distance in front of her. And here she was again, *knowing* — after all, the evidence was quite obvious when she faced the facts — that Sayre was having an affair.

Barbara's thoughts were suddenly interrupted by a startingly loud galloping sound approaching her from behind.

"No! Brutus! No! You get over here right now! Brutus!"

Barbara turned just in time to be greeted by a

112

large, intimidating Rottweiller that circled her, jumping around wildly.

"Don't worry, it's okay, he's just a puppy and he loves people. Don't you, Brutus?"

The dog happily ran back towards his owner who began to pet him playfully. "Really sorry about that, hope he didn't scare you," the woman said to Barbara as she lifted a stick and threw it out toward the ocean. The overgrown puppy raced after it with a cheerful bark.

"Oh, that's okay," Barbara said, relieved that the Rottweiler was only a puppy. She took a moment to appraise the giant puppy's attractive master. There was something about the woman that caught Barbara's attention immediately. Was it her hypnotic eyes, tinted in a hue that seemed to reflect the beauty of the ocean? Her contagious smile that gracefully exposed the even white teeth? Or perhaps it was just her aura of warmth, of caring.

"What a good boy!" the woman yelled to the dog as he tackled the stick and ran down the beach. "That's my cue!" she said to Barbara. "On the beach, *he* leads. *I* follow. See you around." She broke into a run, following her dog who had just disappeared around the bend.

So how do they do it? Barbara wondered, watching the woman as she vanished in pursuit of her dog. For instance, with a woman like her . . . should she have said, "Hey how about an affair this afternoon?" How did these things get started anyway?

Barbara walked down to the edge of the water, reached in her jacket, and threw a small rock she had found earlier that afternoon out into the sea. She stood there maybe ten minutes, maybe twenty, just

thinking about Diane, Sayre, and finally, the pretty
stranger.

She headed further down the beach, lost in
thoughts of how she would approach the woman if
she ran into her again, inventing different scenarios
of how it would be when they tumbled into each
other's arms, after she had said all the perfect things,
no longer Diane's poor ex-lover who had been hurt in
the "most unpleasant of circumstances." No longer
the cuckolded girlfriend of hot Sayre who was
running around with God only knew who. From here
on she would be Barbara — *just taking care of
herself,* the way she should have done a long time
ago!

Between walking and running the last half hour
or so with Brutus, Val felt entitled to a rest. "Out of
shape!" she mumbled to herself as she hiked her way
up the steep side of the sand dune, grateful that she
had finally reached her destination. It had gotten
cooler, cloudier, and she was anticipating the shelter
that the dunes offered from the wind.

"Come on, boy!" she called to Brutus who had
been momentarily distracted by a bold seagull
swooping down near his head.

Brutus barked, attempting to explain to the bird
that this spot was now his territory, or so it seemed
to Val. He raced up the side of the dune, out of
breath himself. Both he and Val collapsed in the cozy
nest-like hollow between the dunes, relieved at last to
be out of the biting wind.

Val untied the hood of her jacket and let it fall

down onto her back. She ran a hand through her hair; her scalp itched from being confined in the warmth of the hood.

She was still thinking about that woman she had seen earlier on the beach. It wasn't like her to obsess about a stranger, especially one she had barely met. She really wasn't exactly sure what intrigued her about the woman. She was attractive, sure, but Val saw lots of attractive women every day. Perhaps it was the look in her eye. Even though their eyes had only met briefly, there had been a sort of desperation, a haunted look that had somehow struck a chord in Val.

And what was wrong with obsessing a bit anyway? She was tired of being "the other woman," having to wait for those few and far between times when her lover could get away from her relationship and spend a few hours with her. Like today, her birthday, and where was her lover? Certainly not with Val! Val had, at first, hinted about wanting to spend the day together, and then been reduced to asking. Then pleading. And finally, enraged that her lover, once again, "probably wouldn't be able to get out," Val had stormed out of the room. "Fine!" she had stammered. "I'll just spend my birthday with Brutus, at the beach — alone!" And even then, she was secretly hoping that her lover would surprise her . . . that she would know, without a doubt, the very place that Val and Brutus would go . . . to the picnic spot in the dunes. Was she being a fool *even at this very instant?* She still thought that at any moment her lover would show up with a bottle of wine, a loaf of bread, perhaps some pâté — and maybe even a small box that held a birthday crystal . . .

She fell back into the sand, closing her eyes, imagining first the fantasy of hearing her lover as she climbed the side of the dune, and then angrily trying to forget her by conjuring up the image of the woman on the beach. Maybe she was coming toward her this very minute, perhaps looking specifically for Val, climbing the dune, taking her into her arms and kissing her passionately.

Suddenly, as if he could read his master's mind, Brutus gave Val a large wet lick across her face.

"Brutus! What a mess!" she said as she wiped the thick, sand-soaked saliva from her face. Brutus put his paws across her chest, wagging his tail excitedly, attempting one more kiss. Val hurled a stick over the side of the dune. "Go get it, boy," she said, protecting her face from the blast of sand as Brutus leaped over the hill and out of sight.

"Brutus, is that you?" Val heard a vaguely familiar voice coming from the other side of the dune. She stood up and peered down the hill in that direction.

"Oh! hello," Val said, feeling a rush of excitement as she saw the woman she had seen earlier on the beach petting Brutus as if they were long lost friends. "Good dog!" she whispered to herself, realizing that her big lug of a buddy had just caught *the* fish of the day on his line.

"Hi!" Barbara responded cheerfully, looking up the side of the hill towards Val. "I was hoping this was Brutus and not some strange dog heading for me!" She bent down to scratch his head. "Isn't that right, Brutus?"

God she was pretty, Val thought as she watched

the woman pull the stick from Brutus's mouth and toss it down the beach. Brutus awkwardly galloped toward the stick. The woman broke into a laugh.

"He's kind of a klutz, huh?" she said, looking back up to Val. She shielded her eyes against the strong wind.

"Yeah, he's a klutz all right!" Val replied as Brutus ran up the hill, kicking sand in all directions. "Wind's pretty chilly. Its getting colder. You're welcome to join me up here until it dies down."

"Sounds great! By the way, I'm Barbara."

"Val."

She ascended the dune. How fortunate that she had found this woman again — after all, she had spent the last half hour with that very goal in mind! But now what? Should she just tell her? Say that she'd been thinking of kissing her since she first saw her on the beach? Barbara slowed her climb up the dune to give her extra time to perfect her plan of action. She'd had lots of ideas wandering down the beach. How come none of them sounded so great now that she was less than four feet away from the object of her fantasy?

"Need some help?" Val asked, extending her hand.

As Barbara reached for Val's outstretched hand, Val gave an extra strong tug. Barbara came rushing up over the top of the dune and fell into the hollow. Val, losing her balance, landed directly on top of Barbara. Brutus, wanting only to be a part of this interesting-looking game, leaped on top of Val causing the women to break into laughter.

"No, Brutus. No!" Val said, trying to create a commanding tone to her voice. "Go lie down . . . lie down right now."

Brutus lumbered off and collapsed a short distance away.

"Good dog!" Val pulled herself off Barbara and smiled. "I was hoping I'd run into you again, but I didn't mean to do it so literally!"

"You know," Barbara said as she propped herself up on her elbows. Okay, here it goes, she thought, now what?

Val was staring at her, waiting for her to complete her sentence — and cute she was, bundled up in that jacket, and those clear, intriguing eyes . . . Val had said that she was hoping to run into her! Go ahead, Barbara thought. Make a move.

"It's just that . . ." Barbara picked up a broken twig and began to draw small circles in the sand. ". . . that, I was hoping I'd run into you too."

Shit! Barbara thought, annoyed with herself. All that practicing, all that talking to myself for the last half hour, to come out with that! *I was hoping I'd run into you too?*

Val just sat there for a moment, looking directly at Barbara, and then quietly said, "Today's my birthday. I'm kind of out celebrating, *all alone*, with Brutus." She let her gaze drift momentarily to the small circles that Barbara was drawing in the sand and then back to Barbara.

Okay, this is it! Barbara thought, not quite able to look up at Val. *Barbara's First Affair:* Take one!

"Can I give you a birthday kiss?" Barbara

murmured shyly, dropping the twig and slowly permitting her eyes to meet Val's.

Val, her cheeks ruddy from the sea breeze, turned and leaned closer to Barbara. "Yes," she answered softly, her lips moving close to Barbara's. "That's exactly what I'd like." She placed her lips softly onto Barbara's.

Barbara closed her eyes as Val's mouth gently touched her own. Oh, how she wanted this woman . . . to be embraced by her, touched by her — to forget all the worrying, all the pain. She moved closer to Val, to let her in — to open her mouth just the smallest bit. Val wanted it, too.

Val immediately responded by taking Barbara into her arms, continuing to kiss her lightly on the lips, on her cool cheeks, her very chilly small nose, her forehead that was slightly protected by the dark brown bangs. She didn't want to stop, wanted only to take in more and more of wonderful Barbara.

Barbara let out a small moan. How very good, how very safe it felt to be with Val. She was wrapped even closer into Val who was nuzzling her face between Barbara's jacket collar and her neck. What a delicious scent Val had about her — all incense and forest. Barbara felt swept away in the moment. Quickly she reached her hands up to Val's face and ran her hands through her hair. The fragrance of evergreen seemed to float out from her dark curls and surround them both.

They kissed fully, deeply, their tongues carefully exploring the sensitive tissues of each others' mouths. A warm tingling sensation shot through Barbara each time the tip of her tongue gently tapped the tip of Val's.

Both women were moaning in pleasure, just from the kissing, just from the very sensuality of their embrace. Val drew back slightly and looked into Barbara's eyes. Barbara took the opportunity to begin unsnapping the buttons on Val's heavy jacket.

"Ever make love at the ocean before?" Barbara asked flirtatiously.

"Well, it's been quite some time," Val answered, pulling off her jacket and laying it in the sand.

"I've heard some nasty rumors about some of the places that sand can travel if you're not careful!" Barbara giggled.

"You just let me take care of that." Val unbuttoned her flannel shirt and placed it alongside her jacket, creating a makeshift blanket. The cold air woke her sleepy nipples, causing them to tighten immediately.

Barbara, taken with the sight of Val's breasts, became even more aroused as she watched the nipples stand at attention.

"Oh!" Barbara exclaimed as she grazed her cold finger across the cold hardened pink but. "You have beautiful breasts."

"Let me see yours, my little pretty!" Val said, twirling an imaginary mustache and then unzipping Barbara's jacket. She leaned over and pulled Barbara's dark green sweatshirt over her head, tossing it next to the coat.

"Very lovely," she murmured. She cupped Barbara's breasts in her hands, lifting them with a most delicate touch, caressing them as though they were porcelain pieces from an expensive collection. Slowly, she began to suck them gently, holding both soft breasts with one hand. Her other hand glided tenderly around Barbara's waist then up to the soft down that filled the hollow of her arm pit. Continuing to pull ever so slightly, her mouth lapped on both the nipples at the same time.

Barbara leaned back, feeling the cold air . . . What a wonderful sensation — her body becoming so warm, out in the open. She could hear the loud roar of the ocean calling in an increasingly demanding rhythm as she felt Val's cool hands unzipping her jeans, struggling to pull them off.

Barbara let out a laugh. "I'll take mine off, you do yours!" She began to tug off her jeans. Standing, she was higher than the dunes that had been acting as a wind barrier. The strong wind hit her face, tousled her hair, chilled her breasts. She turned into the wind and looked out toward the sea; the waves were higher, more powerful than earlier. The beach was empty except for a small figure in the distance heading, or so it appeared, in their direction. Quickly she removed her jeans and sat down.

Shivering, she drew Val into her arms. She liked Val's Rubenesque figure: full breasts, rounded belly, large hips and thighs — the epitome of femininity. She smoothly moved her cool hand down and around Val's breasts, caressing the nipple between her fingers. She hesitated there for a moment and then continued her exploration, moving down over the curved stomach and entering into the wilderness of hair. She combed her fingers gently through the raised nest, marveling at how much hair there actually was. Her hand slowly worked its way down Val's thigh to her knee, feeling the velvet layer of hair that blanketed her skin.

"Barbara," Val sighed as she caressed Barbara's

121

somewhat smaller figure. She buried her face in Barbara's shoulder, luxuriating in the spicy scent of her perspiration. She held on tightly, enjoying Barbara's touch, letting herself float in the pleasures her own body was receiving.

Once again, Barbara slid her hand back up Val's leg to the thick hair that, like an overgrown garden, totally concealed Val's sex. Barbara let her fingers explore their way in through the dense hair and slowly began to search for the crevice that would guide her to Val's treasures.

Val leaned back, allowing her legs to separate further to afford Barbara a chance to find the secreted opening. Barbara inched her finger into the crease and felt it gently slide into the slippery folds of skin. She glided her finger up and slowly down each side of Val's silken pink lady. How wet, how slick the tissues were! What a wonderful sensation to feel the moist heat from Val's pussy as she heard the wind circling above her, outside of the protection of the dune.

Gracefully she kissed her way down Val's shoulders to her full breasts, stopped to lightly suck the nipples, and then moved further down with her lips, across the smooth, soft belly with little kisses, loving kisses, she worked her way to the very place she longed to be . . . at the border of Val's dark, curly thicket of hair.

A moan escaped from Val's lips as Barbara ran her warm tongue into the tangled hair.

"Yes, oh yes. that is so sweet."

Barbara's tongue slipped into the slope between the large outer lips. Val was indeed sweet. The light scent that seemed to be calling to her from deep between those lips was becoming too much to bear. Wanting more, she forced her tongue into the very center, separating those thick lips with her tongue, entering the hot dampness once and for all.

She shifted her position so she could lie between Val's legs and bury her face in the aromatic triangle, cupping and lifting Val's ample ass in her hands, giving her better access to that musky slit.

Val was running her fingers through Barbara's hair, stroking her, as Barbara continued to lightly lap along the sides of her throbbing clitoral shaft.

Barbara was overwhelmed by the enticing tangy taste, the alluring scent that was a mixture of a dew-covered forest floor and a salty breeze. She could not remember ever having been surrounded by such a seductive perfume.

She burrowed her way down to the very center, the very place where that fragrance seemed to emanate from, and flicked her tongue in and out of the rimmed vaginal opening. It was almost as if the tissue around the entrance had a rigid elastic-like ring directly below the skin . . . It was so tight, so ungiving.

Barbara continued to circle her tongue around the raised portal of flesh. She was drunk with pleasure, dipping the tip of her tongue into the sticky sap and then delicately running it up to the shaft. Val's clitoris was erect in anticipation of each delicious stroke as Barbara traveled back down to the succulent well, only to return to the tiny pink kernel. Up and across in a flicking rhythm, returning home to the syrupy opening.

Val writhed in pleasure, pushing her hungry pussy

against Barbara's taut tongue. She let go of Barbara's hair and fondled her own aching nipples, squeezing them sharply while Barbara continued that remarkable tempo at her pussy.

"Don't stop, please Barbara, that's so good," Val uttered in a pleasure-laden voice.

Barbara was more than willing to continue the pace, to meet Val's pussy that seemed to be trying to swallow her tongue. Val's pussy was creaming, lathered up in a froth of sex juice. Barbara felt a driving impulse to take in more and more. Her face submerged between Val's legs, her gentle licking from moments before evolved into a ravenous sucking.

Suddenly, Brutus jumped up with a bark and bounded over the side of the dune, kicking a huge storm of sand onto both of the women.

"Brutus! Damn that dog!" Val said as Barbara pulled up from between her legs.

"Got us both!" Barbara said with a laugh, attempting to brush the layer of sand off Val's belly.

"Wonder what's up with him?" Val stood and peered over the side of the dune. And there he was, not far down the beach, jumping in elated greeting around Val's lover. She was handing him a treat from a small picnic basket.

"Oh shit!" Val moaned, turning to Barbara. "I've got a little problem here and . . ." She was throwing the flannel shirt around herself and trying to get the jeans on. "Somebody's coming . . ." Val pulled up the zipper.

"Let's just be quiet. Certainly they'll just pass on by," Barbara said matter-of-factly, wondering what all the big fuss was about.

"It's not that simple," Val replied nervously, only

to be interrupted by her lover, who was at the bottom of the sand dune.

"Hey, honey, surprised I found you?" the woman below yelled up toward the love nest where both Barbara and Val were scrambling to get dressed — knocking into each other, sand flying everywhere.

"God, I'm sorry!" Val said, seeing that Barbara understood the situation. They bumped each other in their final efforts to cover themselves.

First Brutus came leaping over the sand dune, followed by the picnic basket, and then Val's lover.

Barbara, pulling up her jeans, turned to the woman who had climbed into the small, sex-fragrant nest and stood there with a shocked expression on her face.

"Sayre, I can explain," Barbara said, feeling the wind whipping through her hair, hearing the sound of the ocean as it seemed to call to her.

Val, who was at first only concerned with Sayre, felt her mouth fall open as she turned to Barbara.

"Barbara? You're *that* Barbara?"

Sayre stood there not quite able to speak, staring at the two dishevelled women. Brutus jumped around, nudging their hands, happy to have all his buddies to play with.

Suddenly Barbara realized that Sayre was not here for her . . . not here for her at all! How could Sayre have even known where she was? Sayre hadn't been able to spend the day with her today because a friend had been in an accident — was at the hospital — and here Sayre stood, picnic basket in hand, expecting to find . . . Val was staring wide-eyed at Sayre.

Barbara turned and looked directly at Val. Did she imagine a certain bond between them? A certain final

distaste for Sayre? She thought back to Marlene . . .
about insurance . . . about her choice to no longer
put up with Sayre anymore . . . about her tender
lovemaking with Val who was now turning towards
her, an apologetic expression in her sea-blue eyes.

"Sayre," Barbara said coolly, trying to hold back
all the hurt, all the emotions. "I'm so sorry that you
had to find out about this in *such* an unpleasant
way." She let out a small, quick breath, risking it all
at this very moment, as she took her hand from her
pocket and reached out to Val. "Isn't that right,
Val?"

Val looked back up to Sayre and then over to
Barbara. She let her cool hand fall into the warmth
of Barbara's. "Yes, Barbara. That's *exactly* right."

She squeezed Barbara's hand and then quickly
pulled her as she started to guide Barbara past Sayre,
and down the dune. And in that moment, when she
was directly in front of Sayre, Val stopped briefly,
reaching into the picnic basket and pulling out the
bottle of wine.

"Thanks for the birthday present, Sayre!" she said
sarcastically as she, Barbara and Brutus headed down
the side of the sand dune . . . leaving a speechless
Sayre staring after them.

VICTORIA

I first met Victoria in a clothing shop on Castro. I was trying on a jacket, appraising myself in the mirror, when she spoke to me.

"Looks hot," she said, and when I turned to see who had made the comment, I was quite taken.

She was taller than me, I guess by two inches, around five foot eight. Really built, solid, strong looking, she was leaning against the wall about five feet away, just staring. Her hair was blonde — bleached, actually — short, closely cropped at the sides, but longer on top, pulled up, sort of new wave;

you know the look. That alone was very striking, just her look. But when I looked even closer, I was captivated by her ice-blue eyes.

I'm not sure how long she had been watching me. I had been standing in front of the mirror for quite a while — pulling the collar up, then down, zipping and unzipping the jacket — absorbed in deciding whether I loved the jacket two hundred and eighty-five dollars' worth.

And when she told me the jacket looked hot, I turned and took one more look in the mirror — and you know what? All that time I had been standing there trying to determine if I liked the coat — not knowing, not sure — and all it took was her saying that it looked hot. Suddenly, I looked in the mirror and I felt hot. That's the kind of effect Victoria had on me from the very start.

She walked over to me, adjusted the collar and shoulders, turned me toward the mirror, and stood almost directly behind me. I could see the reflection of her face to the right of my own and feel her hands on my shoulders.

"Yes," she said evenly. "That's the look — yeah, hands in the pockets, collar up. That jacket, and a little of that attitude right there could open up a whole new world to you."

Needless to say, within minutes I was the owner of that suede jacket and was walking out of the store with it on — collar up, hands in pockets, full of, if I do say so myself, a very hot new attitude. Victoria walked out beside me, told me her name, and asked where I was headed. At that point, I hadn't any plans. After my two-hundred-and-eighty-five-dollar expenditure, my shopping spree had come to a sudden halt.

I turned toward Victoria. In the sunlight, she was even prettier. Her creamy complexion was smooth as glass — a marked contrast to her black turtleneck tank top. And as she spoke, I caught the dance of tiny sparkles that seemed to be sprinkled around her ear. They were small diamond studs that began at her earlobe and followed each other up the outer rim of her ear. God, she was stunning!

"I'm meeting a friend of mine for tea," she continued, the sunlight still skipping about on her diamond-lined ear, creating a rainbow of colors. "Come join us! At the Starlight Cafe, you know, on Polk."

I stood, somewhat transfixed by this masterpiece of a woman and quickly answered, "Yes."

I debated taking my own car, but Victoria convinced me, without too much resistance on my part, that we'd be better off in one car — hers.

Within twenty minutes we were in the Starlight Cafe. A woman with long, full, dark hair waved to us from the back corner of the restaurant. Victoria grabbed my arm and pulled me along.

"Rose, this is Andrea," Victoria said quickly as we reached the booth. I sat down next to her.

Looking back on the whole thing, it's hard to say who was prettier — Andrea with her feminine, soft features, or Victoria with her tough, vivid beauty. Either way, I was totally mesmerized by them both.

They began talking about this and that. I felt a little strange to be there, not really knowing either of them. So I sat there, not paying much attention to the conversation, watching Andrea's thick, full lips as she spoke.

It was fascinating — with some words, her lips would form a small heart. Occasionally, I could see her pink tongue dart in and out. Then she would laugh, transforming that perfect heart into a diamond, then a circle. And all the while, that tease of a tongue would be flicking back and forth, in and out.

"We'd really like you to come watch, what do you think?" I heard Victoria saying to me as she gave me a slight nudge, bringing me back from my fantasy paradise where Andrea's pink lips were on my own.

I was more than embarrassed, feeling my face suddenly grow warm — totally unaware of the conversation. "Sure, sounds great!" I answered, trying to sound as if I had been listening all along.

"Great!" Victoria responded with enthusiasm. "Why don't we all go over in my car. Andrea, take care of the bill — we'll get the car."

Andrea gave me a slight wink and an incredibly seductive smile with those inviting lips. "See you out front," she said.

Had I imagined the innuendo in her words?

"Andrea will blow you away," Victoria said, grabbing my arm and leading me down Polk, toward the car. She opened the door and I quickly slid in.

The apartment was only five minutes away and I'm not sure why we didn't just walk, but we arrived there barely after I had buckled my seat belt.

The downstairs apartment was off an alley between two buildings. The alley was narrow and dark, and as we entered, I had the sudden feeling of being trapped. I turned to say something to this effect and realized I was sandwiched between two exceptional women, and that I was being quite dreary — bordering on being a stick-in-the-mud. We were only going into an alley to an apartment. I reached up and allowed my fingers to caress my new suede jacket, urging myself to take on the hot attitude that wearing an expensive jacket like this entitled me to. I adjusted the collar, put my shoulders back and followed Victoria into a small studio apartment.

Like the alley we had just escaped from, the apartment was cool, dark and shadowy. Andrea went directly into the bathroom where a light burned and closed the door, dissipating the shadows.

Victoria turned on a very small lamp, creating an amber glow throughout the room.

"Make yourself comfortable," she said matter-of-factly, pulling a leather chair closer into the center of the room and motioning for me to sit.

I started to remove the suede jacket but stopped when Victoria said, "Oh no. Leave the jacket on. That's what this is all about, Rose."

"Oh yes, of course," I answered hesitantly, wishing I had paid more attention to the conversation at the cafe and less attention to Andrea's lips.

"I want you to sit here and not say a word unless I tell you to speak," Victoria said, her voice deeper, more direct.

I gave her a slight nod, seating myself in the chair, wondering what I was in for. But my thoughts were abruptly interrupted by the sound of the bathroom door opening. And there in the doorway stood Andrea, the soft bathroom light surrounding her like a spotlight.

I doubt there are words to accurately describe how

Andrea looked, standing in that doorway — and the incredible effect she had on me.

Her hair was pulled back, and she had put a muted rose-colored blush on her cheeks; her face had an amazing union of seductiveness and vulnerability. She was wearing a black satin slip that seemed to angrily contrast her pale pink skin. The lace bodice barely covered her full breasts.

She just stood there quietly, as though waiting to be asked into the room. She stared directly at me. There was a different quality about her now — a sort of new accessibility I hadn't noticed before.

A sudden movement drew my attention away from Andrea. Victoria had dragged a leather footrest to the center of the room. She looked over at me and then to Andrea.

"You may enter now, Andrea," she said, her voice edged with an unfamiliar tone.

Andrea slowly approached Victoria. When she was almost directly in front of her, Victoria gently took Andrea into her arms and lovingly began to kiss her.

It was arousing to sit in the chair and watch those two beauties kissing. I was close enough that I could actually see Victoria's tongue gently outlining those succulent, full lips of Andrea's. I could hear Andrea moan very slightly in response.

"Yes," Victoria was saying softly, "Yes, my beauty. Now is the time."

And without a word, Andrea got on her knees and bent over the large leather footrest.

From my point of view, I could see quite clearly the back of Andrea's firm thighs, her high, round ass propped up in the air in front of me, and part of her nicely shaped back.

There was something extremely erotic about seeing Andrea in this position — the slip raised just enough to expose her arched-up, heart-shaped ass. She was like a piece of artwork at a museum — on display, to be gazed upon, thought about, appreciated.

Victoria walked over to the couch and pulled a small case from beneath it. She lifted the lid and carefully removed a fairly long, thick peacock feather.

As though silently responding to Victoria's movements, Andrea's ass pushed higher into the air, as if straining to keep a tension throughout her body. A tension that began in that taut, forced up ass.

Victoria walked over to me and leaned down so close I could take in the light scent of her perfume and perspiration innocently intertwined.

"It's a very simple technique," she whispered smoothly, a cool tone in her voice. "You start it off light, gently, and then as her body responds, you increase to her needs."

I was rather confused as to what my reaction to all this should be. I was beginning to realize what I was about to witness . . . and I was very aware of my mixed feelings. Part of me wanted to leave immediately. I had never been interested in what I considered "loveless sex." And voyeurism fell into that category as far as I was concerned. I'd had three lovers in my life — and each relationship was long-term. So sitting here, realizing that perhaps I was getting into something that I normally viewed as distasteful, made me feel quite uncomfortable.

And yet, there was another side of me that was totally mesmerized by the vision of Andrea — her ass so yielding and vulnerable, the idea of that thick feather lightly moving across those fleshy cheeks —

perhaps causing that full ass to jut even further out from beneath that satin curtain of a slip . . . I felt an intense tingling in my pussy at just the thought of it!

So it was quite clear to me that I wasn't going anywhere at all. Planted, almost cemented to the chair, I listened to Victoria speak, allowing her fragrance to invade my own tightly bound senses.

She moved back over to Andrea and began to lightly graze the back of Andrea's thighs with the peacock feather. She caressed the high, round cheek on the right, then lightly brushed it across the left cheek. Running that full fluffy tip in small circles back and forth, she gently moved it between her thighs, which involuntarily spread apart — affording me quite a look at that bushy thatch of hair that densely covered her full, thick pussy. Victoria stroked the feather up and down her crotch — poking the feather, vibrating it. I could hear Andrea moan, pushing her ass up as if pleading for much, much more.

I sat in awe. I had never seen such a thing! The part of me that only a few minutes before had considered leaving was totally engrossed in the scene I was witnessing. Andrea was silent. The only reaction I could observe was her ass arching in pleasure.

Victoria tossed the feather toward the couch and slowly fell to her knees not quite in front of Andrea's voluptuous ass. She was whispering — but loud enough for me to hear. "Oh baby, the finest ass, the finest ass — that's what you have, isn't it? Do you like to show it off? Do you like knowing that she's sitting across the room watching you flaunt it?"

I stared.

"That's right, baby," Victoria continued, her voice more audible. "Let me slip one finger in — just enough. Just enough so we can let her know what you've really got here."

I was stunned, unable to move, spellbound with feelings of sexual heat and desire. My entire body was tensed up, on edge.

"Rose," Victoria murmured, turning to me. "I want you to stick your tongue out. I want you to taste perhaps the finest pussy you'll ever, *ever* taste."

Still entranced, I stiffened in the chair and leaned forward — remembering not to leave the chair, as Victoria had instructed when this scene started — desperate to get to that glistening finger as quickly as possible.

"That's right, Rose," Victoria said hypnotically. "Come and get some."

Victoria was directly in front of me holding that juicy finger right beneath my nose, intoxicating me with that most wondrous scent.

I put my tongue out, impatient for the taste. Would it be sweet? Tart? I felt the saliva in my mouth welling up in anticipation.

Carefully, Victoria slid her finger onto my waiting tongue. I enveloped that finger, blanketing it. Then slowly I closed my lips and began sucking it, greedily trying to remove every last drop of that delicious confectionery taste.

"Now, now," Victoria teased, chastening me. "There's much more . . . you'll have to let me have my finger though."

Reluctantly, I let go, not realizing I had such a demanding grip on that nectar-courier of a finger.

I began to feel the moisture between my own legs. I could not believe how excited I had become. There was an insistent throbbing directly in the heart of my pussy. I squirmed slightly in the chair, accidentally letting out a small moan.

I found myself perched on the edge of my chair, leaning forward, trying to soak in that thick air of sweat and alluring scents coming from the center of the room.

Victoria turned to me. "Do you want her?" she said, taking my hand and leading me over to Andrea.

I was so hot, so aroused. I felt as though she had pulled me through a tantalizing, sticky film into a web of sexual passion.

"Lift up, Andrea," she said coolly. "Lift up that perfect ass of yours and spread your legs so Rose can make up her mind if she wants you!"

Andrea immediately arched her ass up even higher, spreading her legs as she did so, exposing her tulip-like pussy lips creaming in sex juice.

"Is that what you want, Rose?" Victoria asked as she walked back to the case and pulled out a long, black dildo with a black leather harness attached to it.

"Stick your fingers in her, Rose," Victoria urged. "Feel how wet Andrea can get!"

I was overwhelmed. I stood in front of Andrea's ass and stared. The air was thick with sex fragrances.

Victoria took my hand and guided it to those petal-like lips. My fingers were engulfed in the damp warmth of her softness.

"I want you to fuck her with this," Victoria said, unsnapping my pants and pulling them off. I didn't move. I just stood there, slowly turning my fingers in that slippery, yielding sex pocket.

Victoria slid the black harness up my legs and around my waist.

It was strange to look down and see the large, dark rod with its smooth, bulbous head dangling below my own slightly curved stomach. With my free hand, I reached up and touched the dildo — it was veined, full of ridges — like a real penis would be on a rather well-endowed man.

"Fuck her!" Victoria said hotly. She grabbed two pillows and slid them under Andrea — causing her to lift higher, giving me direct access to her puffed-out pussy.

I caressed the tip of the large, black cock until it was lubricated with Andrea's slippery juices. Then I grabbed each side of her hips and began to slowly insert the large head into her hungry slit. She was tight, small. I wasn't sure if it would go in — she was moaning, squirming a bit.

"Go ahead, give it to her," Victoria panted behind me. She grabbed my hips and thrust them forward, causing that big dildo to slam into Andrea. Quickly, she pulled my hips back, tugging the dildo out. I looked down; the large rim of the head had just slid out of that tight, stretched opening. Abruptly, Victoria jammed my hips forward again. I saw the large dildo pry its way back in. Again Victoria moved my hips back slowly and I watched that slick rod drag back out of her bright red orifice.

"Now. You got it?" Victoria said. "You fuck her. Let me watch." Her ice-blue eyes were piercing and direct.

I leaned forward. Did I imagine the sucking sound as I forced the dildo back into Andrea and pulled it out again?

"Faster!" Victoria insisted. She circled around us.

I increased the speed. Andrea began to move her hips, rotating them around and around as I slid that ribbed cock in and out.

Victoria picked up the peacock feather and gave Andrea a quick brush on the ass, causing her to lunge off the thick cock. "Come on, come on," Victoria moaned, continuing to brush Andrea's ass with the feather.

Greedily, I moved back into her, holding her hips more securely, sinking into her. The sound of the slapping noise each time I entered Andrea, her moans as I watched her ass gyrate, hungrily sucking in that large tool, excited me even more.

I increased my rhythm to meet Victoria's coaxing. I felt hot, steeped in some sort of paradise. Watching Andrea's ass twirling around, watching her pussy mouthing that large cock, I was taken in! Caught up! Overwhelmed with desire!

"Get on the floor! Get on the floor now!" Victoria said. She positioned us cunt to cunt, side by side on the floor.

"Spread your legs," she insisted as she pulled a long, double-ended dildo from her case. In a second, she had inserted one end into Andrea and one end into me.

Andrea started moving at once — tightening her legs up near my waist. Each time she moved, the other end of the dildo pushed into me.

Victoria squatted next to us and began manipulating both our clitorises at the same time.

"Now," she said, "here we go."

Her expert fingers filled me with the most incredible pleasure. My clitoris was pounding in direct response to her constant motion.

Within seconds, I was arching up, slamming down onto that dildo — no longer certain of Andrea's movements — only aware of that dildo ramming into me over and over.

"Nice, baby, nice," Victoria was saying smoothly — continually bouncing my clit back and forth.

I burst into a conquering orgasm that had me racked in pleasure, jamming that dildo — fucking it — imagining Andrea on the other end — causing resistance with her tight, tight pussy. I had visions of Victoria with the diamond studs — adjusting my jacket collar in the store — telling me how hot I looked. Surrounded by Andrea's scent, feeling the heat of my new jacket around me, I arched into ecstasy.

I came hard. So hard I was screaming, "Yes, oh yes, Victoria! You make me hot! So, so hot!"

My body tightened and then suddenly I relaxed, totally spent.

I opened my eyes. Victoria was sitting on the floor, leaning up against the couch — inhaling slowly from her cigarette.

"Yeah," she said with a sexy smile. "That jacket and a little of that attitude right there could open a whole new world to you."

MARGEAUX

Margeaux restlessly tossed in her bed, yanked the powder blue sheet from over her head and peered across the darkened room at the glow of the clock. Twelve thirty a.m. She had been trying to fall asleep for almost an hour and a half, to no avail. The nights that Sarah worked graveyard shift dragged — always the same restless nights. She tried to sleep, or at least relax, but could never do much of either.

Margeaux loved Sarah, loved her so completely that when they were together nothing else seemed to matter. But lately, Margeaux's long, lonely nights had been haunted by memories of Sonya. It had been six months since Sonya and Margeaux had broken up, and as Margeaux knew quite well, it was the best thing that could have happened to that stormy, agitated relationship.

And yet, Margeaux once again thought as she sat up in the large, half-empty bed, along with the anger and fighting was the intense passion and fire . . .

"I hate it," Margeaux whispered aloud, noting her hazy reflection in the mirror. "I hate it when Sarah's not here." The other side of the bed seemed so cold, so vast without the heat from her warm-bodied partner.

. . . And then, Sonya sometimes would force her against the wall and in anger rip open her blouse. "You are so selfish!" she'd scream, her eyes flashing, pressing Margeaux against the wall.

Margeaux reached to the night table and turned on the antique beaded lamp.

If only I could see Sonya one more time, she thought, closing her eyes, preparing to recreate the fantasy of showing up at Sonya's door late at night, a surprise visit.

Suddenly, Margeaux felt a rush of energy pass through her — as if some sort of magic dust had surrounded her, changing her entire perspective, changing everything about the long night.

Margeaux got out of bed, stepped into the pearl-white satin nightgown that she had let fall to the floor earlier, walked as if in a trance to her dressing table, and sprayed a hint of Sonya's favorite fragrance between her breasts. A dash of shadow above her dark eyes and a blush of ruby red on her lips completed the picture.

She stepped back, appraising herself in the mirror, running her hands up and down the smooth satin gown that clung to her soft, perfumed body.

Yes, she thought, feeling a stirring deep in her heart, "Tonight." She shivered, though the summer night was hot and arid.

Barefoot, not taking the time to find her shoes or robe, Margeaux found herself outside, in the car, on the freeway to Sonya's house. It would be hours before Sarah would be home. Margeaux had plenty of time to take care of this fantasy that had been robbing her of her sleep.

The twenty-minute ride went by quickly. At one a.m., the roads were lonely, empty, like the other half of Margeaux's bed when Sarah was working that damned graveyard shift.

Clicking off the car headlights, Margeaux turned onto the gravel drive that led to Sonya's house. Out in the country the air smelled fresh, alive. Margeaux could see the outline of Sonya's bungalow in the light of the moon. Stopping the car, Margeaux sat, staring at the darkened home, hearing only the sound of her own deep breathing. Surrounded by darkness, yet enveloped in the light of the moon, she let her whole body savor the moment.

Margeaux opened the car door and hurried toward the wooden steps that would usher her to Sonya's door. She knocked.

"Who . . . Who is it?" Sonya's sleepy voice demanded from behind the door.

Margeaux, still entranced, couldn't seem to talk. Part of her was wondering what the hell she was doing here. What would Sarah think? Better yet, what would Sonya do after not having had any contact, after that last argument, after . . .

"I said who is it!" Sonya's voice was stronger, familiar.

"Me," whispered Margeaux, barely audible. "Me, me, me!" she said, not moving, barely breathing.

Immediately, the door opened and Sonya stood directly in front of Margeaux. "Well, what do you know!" she said, quickly pulling Margeaux into the dark house, closing the door.

"I . . . I . . ." Margeaux stammered, not having a chance to answer as Sonya turned on a tiny light in the front room.

"And who, *who* in the hell do you think you are, just showing up? What are you doing here? Where's your wonderful lover Sarah?" Sonya demanded, briskly asking one question, then the next, all the while appraising Margeaux's bare feet, the outline of her large nipples pushing against the satin gown, her red wild hair and ruby lips.

Taken with what she saw, with the image Margeaux presented, Sonya grabbed Margeaux's arm and whisked her into the bedroom, onto the bed.

Margeaux felt herself falling onto Sonya's soft, hot waterbed. The waves resisted her and then moved with her. Sonya stood in the moonlight above her. The scent of her was already causing Margeaux to pant ever so slightly.

"You think after six months, at your slightest whim, you can just show up at my door?" Sonya was whispering, yet her anger was evident. "What do you think I am? At your beck and call? When you want me I'll be here?" The tone was not unfamiliar to Margeaux, who also had mixed emotions.

Yes, she thought, what am I doing? Yet at the same time she could feel every cell in her body liven with anticipation, waiting for the moment when Sonya's anger would break into passion.

Margeaux was swept away by the sight of Sonya standing above her; she exuded strength, anger, confidence, authority. Margeaux tried to raise herself from the bed. She wanted to put her arms around Sonya, make contact, to delight in, to become one with this marvelous powerhouse of a woman.

As Margeaux began to wrap her arms around Sonya's waist, Sonya pushed her away, simultaneously grabbing one of the thin satin straps on Margeaux's peignoir, ripping the satin gown away from Margeaux's soft, patient breasts.

"Mine." Sonya forced Margeaux back onto the bed. Grasping Margeaux's beautiful, full breasts she said, "Oh, you can be with as many women as you want, but you'll always come back to me. I know you, woman." Sonya's voice was a deep monotone. "Like no other ever will! Say it! Say that I own you."

"You own me," Margeaux whispered, shuddering with desire, feeling Sonya's forceful fingers on her breasts, on her rounded belly, rushing through her hair.

"Yes, that's right," Sonya said softly. "You're mine, mine, mine."

Sonya pulled the shredded negligee over Margeaux's hips, down her legs — exposing all of her feminine beauty to Sonya's eyes.

Subtly, the room began to fill with the familiar musky scent of Margeaux's womanhood. Sonya could hardly keep from forcing her face into Margeaux's thick mound of dark hair. Wanting to take her time, yet feeling overwhelmed with urgency, Sonya quickened her pace — moving her face slowly down toward the very center of the fine fragrance that lured her.

"Oh, oh Sonya," Margeaux sighed. "I've missed you. I've missed your touch."

"Yes. Oh yes," Sonya responded as her tongue reached the border of Margeaux's dark forest. "Yes, my love. I've missed you too."

Sonya's tongue began to slowly travel into the forest, parting the soft hair, making a pathway; her lovemaking was so very new — yet so very familiar.

Within seconds, Sonya felt her tongue move out from the entwined hairs and down into the smooth, sleek flesh of Margeaux's fragrant sex. As if she were a thirsty hiker who finally came upon a stream of fresh, cool water, Sonya's tongue began to lap hungrily.

Margeaux purred as Sonya's tongue slowly, yet firmly moved up and down each side of Margeaux's taut clitoris.

"Sonya, oh please, Sonya." Margeaux was lost in sensation.

"That's right, sweet one, that's right, let me hear you moan," Sonya murmured, lifting her face from the luscious forest, watching Margeaux purring, panting, slightly arching.

What a marvelous sight Margeaux was! Six months without her and still no other woman, no other fantasy could compare to Margeaux's soft, curved hips, her beautiful round belly and pert, responsive nipples, her scent . . .

"Sonya, please." Margeaux's urging brought Sonya back from the trance. "You know what I need . . . It's been so long . . . No one, no one knows how to do what you do for me. Oh please baby, I need . . ."

"Oh, is that right!" Sonya interrupted abruptly. "Poor, poor Margeaux has herself a new lover, a whole new life . . . but can't be pleased like I please her." Sonya pulled herself up from between Margeaux's legs and walked over to the closet.

"Sometimes, Margeaux, I'm not quite sure what to do about you. Women like you — you know, spoiled women like you — need to be taught that not everyone in the whole world is willing to be at their beck and call."

"I didn't mean to offend you, make you angry by coming here tonight. I thought you'd be —"

"You thought I'd be what? You self-centered princess!" Sonya snapped angrily. She strode back across the room and pushed Margeaux, who had risen from the bed, hard against the wall.

"I've had it with you . . . coming here without a thought for my feelings! Sneaking around on your lover. What would lovely Sarah think if she knew you were here? Perhaps I should leave a mark so she'll know *exactly* who really owns pretty Margeaux!"

Sonya latched her lips against Margeaux's slim porcelain-like neck and began sucking forcefully.

The room was dark, except for the light of the moon streaming in the large bedroom window. Margeaux, still pinned against the wall, stunned from

146

Sonya's harsh words and strong lips, felt a new, even more urgent rush of electricity go through her.

Her neck stung where Sonya had been sucking. What if there were marks? What in heaven's name would she tell Sarah? Soft, caring Sarah, Margeaux knew, would stand with her face in her hands — tears flowing.

"What's the problem, girlie," Sonya said sarcastically. A smug expression was quite evident on her face, her eyes full of fire. Grabbing a handful of Margeaux's thick red hair in one hand, simultaneously forcing two of her fingers into Margeaux's tight, slippery opening.

"I know what you want," she said, tightening her hold on Margeaux's hair, beginning to work her fingers in and out, in and out of Margeaux's vagina.

Margeaux's scalp ached. She couldn't turn her head. Sonya's face wasn't even an inch from hers. She stung, she ached, and yet the very place where Sonya was forcing her fingers — so roughly, so abruptly — was wet, begging for more.

The room was quiet except for Margeaux's moans and the slapping sound from Sonya driving her fingers into Margeaux; Sonya's palm hit against Margeaux's fleshy folds as she plunged her fingers in over and over.

Sonya herself was more than excited. With each penetration into Margeaux's tight vagina, Sonya became more and more aroused.

"Never anyone like you," Sonya muttered. "Woman, your cunt, the way you feel."

Margeaux was starting to lose control, moaning loudly, arching and tightening all at once. Sonya recognized exactly what this meant, exactly where Margeaux was in her pleasure.

Sonya stopped, lifted Margeaux into her arms and carried her back to the bed. Margeaux was begging, crying, purring, moaning. Pushing her heels into the wood bed frame, she arched her pelvis up.

Sonya, overcome herself with desire, knelt on the bed, turning Margeaux over, pulling Margeaux's arching pelvis down onto her face.

"Ride me!" Sonya demanded, positioning herself beneath Margeaux.

Straddling Sonya's face, Margeaux placed her throbbing clitoris directly over Sonya's ready mouth. Slowly at first, Margeaux began to slide up and down over Sonya's wide, flat tongue. The room smelled of Margeaux and Sonya's scents intertwined. Margeaux was slippery, wet, throbbing — as was Sonya.

As Margeaux slid herself up across Sonya's face, Sonya responded eagerly, putting her tongue, her chin, her nose into Margeaux's delicious pussy. Back and forth Margeaux moved, quickening her pace with each few strokes. Sonya, engulfed by Margeaux, was beyond control herself. Reaching down between her own legs, she quickly began to massage her own bead-like clitoris. As Margeaux increased her pace, so Sonya increased her stroke across her own thick shaft. Faster, faster until suddenly Margeaux was tightening, barely moving. Moaning. Screaming.

It was too much. Feeling Margeaux above her — Margeaux's ruby lips slipping back and forth over Sonya's face, the familiar tightening as Margeaux reached orgasm — Sonya beat her fingers back and forth rapidly. The scent, the fleshy folds, Margeaux's screams of pleasure . . . immediately, Sonya herself

148

was arching in ecstasy, barely able to breathe, Margeaux's soft pussy flush up against her face. The demanding beat of her own fingers continued back and forth, over and over across her hardened shaft.

Sonya grabbed Margeaux's full, soft buttocks as she reached orgasm — pushing Margeaux, forcing Margeaux, clamping Margeaux's pussy to her face. Sonya plunged, driving her tongue deeper and deeper — burrowing, burying, submerging her chin, her nose. Her entire face was slick, glazed with Margeaux's sweet juices.

Pulling out of the throes of her own pleasure, Margeaux became distinctly aware of Sonya's strong fingers digging into the soft flesh of her buttocks. As she tried to shift ever so slightly, she heard Sonya's deep guttural moan, muffled only by her own damp pussy directly against Sonya's mouth.

Suddenly Sonya flipped Margeaux onto her back. In the same movement Sonya rolled on top of Margeaux. Her face saturated in Margeaux's sweet scent, grabbing Margeaux, hugging her, Sonya slid her face against Margeaux's smooth cheek and ran her hands through Margeaux's wild mane, recklessly kissing her over and over.

"Oh baby, my sweet, sweet baby," she murmured, continuing to kiss, hold, melt into Margeaux's very being.

Margeaux grasped tightly onto Sonya — wrapping her arms and legs around Sonya. Two became one, clamped tight, pressed into each other.

Margeaux jumped, startled by the first ring of the telephone. Her heart raced — from the delicious sex, from the suddenness of the phone's sharp ringing.

Margeaux could hardly breathe as she reached

149

over, picked up the receiver, and clicked on the antique beaded lamp by her bed.

"Hello," she gasped.

"Well, hello there sweetie," the familiar voice responded.

"Sarah!" Margeaux whispered, leaning back into her bed, glancing at the clock — twelve forty-five a.m.

"I couldn't help calling. I hope I didn't wake you . . . I just miss you so much when I work graveyard shift!"

"Oh baby, I miss you, too." Margeaux brought her damp fingers up to her nose to enjoy her scent, still fresh on her fingers. Smiling to herself, pressing the cool receiver against her warm face, Margeaux closed her eyes and listened contentedly to the woman she loved so completely.

JESSE

Jesse leaned forward in her chair letting a rather large yawn escape her lips. She glanced over at the wall clock hanging to the right of the message boxes — seven thirty-two PM. Thursday. This wasn't a bad job, really, not compared to some of the things her friends did to earn a few bucks to live on. But when it was as slow as it had been the last few nights — since the resort had opened for the season — well, that's when the hours seemed to drag by.

She was looking forward to this weekend, though.

Tomorrow was the beginning of June . . . and that's when action would begin at Willow Springs Resort!

She thought back to last year. There had been all the different types of women from just about any part of California you could name. That's when being a lesbian and working in an all-women's resort was too good to be true!

But that doesn't really help me tonight, she thought. Jesse leaned back in her chair, bringing her legs up across the front counter. She was already bored. Nothing. Not one tourist, not one call . . . just Jesse, the clock and the old two-station TV. She glanced distractedly over to the black and white television on a small table in the corner, debating whether to click it on or not.

A motorcycle pulled up to the main entrance. "Bev!" she said aloud, with a smile. At least now she'd have some company to help pass the time. Jesse jumped out of the chair and hurried over to the screen door to greet her favorite buddy.

"Hello, lady! Whatcha up to?" Jesse encircled Bev in her arms, not hiding her pleasure in the impromptu visit.

"Aah, not much, just riding around waiting for this town to wake up." Bev gave Jesse a tight hug.

"Hey, tomorrow's the day when people start arriving!" Jesse answered quickly, trying to sound optimistic.

"Oh come on, Jesse, we go through this every year. We both know the first week or so is slow, just the overnighters. The real fun won't start till the reservation ladies show up. Now you tell me you got some of them lined up in your roster and maybe I'll be a little more enthusiastic."

"Okay, okay, not till the eighteenth . . . "

"That's what I thought. Pretty boring here, just sitting in an empty lobby, hoping for a guest to show."

"It does seem like I watch the clock quite a bit," Jesse said, shrugging as she walked back over to her chair. "But at least I've got your company."

"Nope, sorry my dear, I've got myself a date lined up with Marcie tonight. Meeting her over at the Dalton Inn."

"Oh that's just great, another night of staring at the TV," Jesse said with an exaggerated sigh.

"Well, that's the reason I stopped by," Bev said with a grin, pulling a paperback book from her back pocket. "Here, got something for you. *This* is going to take your mind off being here all alone with nothing happening. Marcie turned me on to it . . ." She tossed the book onto the counter.

"Oh come on, Bev! You know I'm not a reader!" She glanced down at the title and then back to Bev. "Especially one with a name like this. I don't go for that summer vacation romance shit!"

"Hey, how often do you see me recommending books to my friends? Trust me on this . . . I think you're going to enjoy this book."

Bev took a brief look at the wall clock. "Whoa! Getting late, gotta run. Enjoy your night!" She gave Jesse a light kiss on the cheek and left. Within seconds the motorcycle was revved up and pulling out of the drive.

Jesse picked up the book, took another look at the clock. "Oh what the hell," she said.

"Excuse me. I *said*, excuse me!"

Jesse, engrossed in the book, looked up in surprise at a very attractive woman standing on the other side of the counter.

"Oh, so sorry," Jesse stammered, embarrassed that she had been caught so off guard. "Can I help you?"

"Well, yes, I should certainly hope so! I need a room for the night . . . and I'm not particularly fond of having to wait to get an employee's attention!

Oh shit, this is all I need, Jesse thought as she pulled the registration form from the top drawer.

"So very sorry," Jesse murmured sweetly, trying to keep the sarcastic edge out of her voice.

She handed the form to the woman who immediately began to fill it out with a gold pen she had taken out of her Gucci bag.

Jesse couldn't help being curious about this woman who was putting information on the form as if it were a major inconvenience.

"You realize, young lady, that I could have had this already completed if you had been doing your job the way I assume your employer expects you to do it!"

What a bitch! Jesse thought, choosing not to answer, but appraising the woman carefully.

There was the Gucci bag for starters . . . and that pen certainly appeared to be fourteen-K. The dark red hair was drawn up in a tight French twist and the outfit was some sort of a designer business suit. This

154

lady was *obviously* just passing through Willow Springs.

"How many nights?" Jesse asked, her voice all sugar.

"One. One occupant, one night . . . and I'll need a quiet room. I have a tremendous amount of work to do tonight and I must *not* be disturbed! Do you understand?"

"Yes Ma'am," Jesse responded with a smile. "I've got the perfect room for you." She reached for the key to room number four. "This room is right behind the front office, no one goes back there. I think it will meet with your satisfaction. Can I give you a hand with your bags?"

"Well, I should think so."

"Great, Ms. Tarree," Jesse said, quickly eyeing the name on the registration slip. Alex Tarree . . . uptown name for sure. It figured, the first lodger of the season had to be some uptight holier-than-thou type. *No* problem! Jesse thought as she led Ms. Tarree out the door and around to the back. Room four was going to meet with everyone's satisfaction tonight!

"Here we are," Jesse opened the door and clicked on the light. "Now if you have any problems, any problems at all — " She walked over to the full-length mirror and switched on the floor lamp next to it. "You be sure to let me know. I'm at your service." Jesse glanced into the mirror. She could see Ms. Tarree looking somewhat impatiently around the room.

"Yes. Thank you. Now if you don't mind, I do have quite a bit of work . . ."

Jesse turned away from the mirror with a smile.

"See you later." She walked past Ms. Tarree to the door.

"Fine." Ms. Tarree said, handing Jesse a dollar bill. "Good evening."

She watched Jesse exit the room, closing the door behind her. "Well, I'm glad that's all over with," she said aloud, unbuttoning her suit jacket.

It had been a long day; the merger meeting with Donald Harris had been draining to say the least. Things looked good for her company, though. It was hard to believe she had only started her business six years ago. How fast things were developing! And Donald Harris meant big money if she could close this deal.

How fortunate that she had found this little inn on the way back to L.A. She was too tired to drive any further . . . and this place was really quite cozy.

She looked in the mirror, removing a large comb from her hair, allowing the French twist to cascade into a waterfall of curls around her face. "I *like* the mirror," she murmured, removing the navy blue suit jacket. She stood by the bed, unzipping the tight blue skirt. She looked quite good, really; almost forty-five, and her body was still in shape — it should be after five days a week at the damned gym. She watched herself pulling the skirt down over her thighs, letting it slowly fall to the floor. A jade green garter belt held up the dark, thigh-high stockings. She liked wearing a garter belt. It made her feel sexy . . . knowing that when she was in some very important meeting looking quite the businesswoman, no one had any idea that she was not wearing panties — just stockings, a garter belt and a lacy little camisole. Now that's what *she* considered hot.

Slowly, she returned to the mirror, carefully undoing the small dark buttons on her expensive white blouse. And with each button that she unfastened, she could see just a hint more of the camisole. Watching attentively, she gradually revealed even more of the seductive lingerie . . . That wonderful full length mirror extended all the way to the floor. She pulled her blouse open; her reflection seemed to tease her . . . those dark stockings melting into the spiked high heels, the sexy little garter belt . . . Oh yes, she had plenty of work to do tonight . . .

Back in the lobby, Jesse relaxed in her favorite position — feet up, chair balancing on two legs. She picked up the book Bev had brought and began to finish the story she had begun reading earlier . . . before she was interrupted by the snippy Ms. Tarree. The nerve of that woman, just because she had some money, or looks, or whatever it was that made her think she was such a princess.

She wanted to continue reading, the story was really quite good so far, but the thought of Ms. Tarree — probably unwinding, perhaps undressing at this very minute — was too much for her. She had been instructed that room four was off-limits for renting out, and had done a most rebellious act by offering it to Ms. Tarree — one that could undoubtedly cost her her job — but these were special circumstances. Surely that was evident. Who'd find out anyway? It would be just her little secret.

Jesse tried to concentrate on the words that were waiting patiently for her. It was too much to ask, to expect of anyone, not to use room four. How could she not take advantage of a situation like this? She really didn't think she could stand it much longer.

Without another thought, she got out of the chair, went into the back office and pulled the full-length drape to one side. And there, directly on the other side of that two-way mirror, was Ms. Tarree . . . and what a sight she was. She stood in front of the mirror wearing only a blouse that was partially open, exposing a lacy satin camisole, a dark green garter belt expertly holding up stockings on those long legs, and a pair of high-heeled shoes that pushed Ms. Tarree's curved calves up quite dramatically. She was watching herself in the mirror as she slowly unbuttoned her blouse.

Jesse let out a low whistle. She hadn't known, hadn't really considered what she would see when she pulled aside the heavy curtain. She had never broken a rule at work before, never even considered renting out room four, but there was something about Ms. Tarree that warranted this type of behavior. That attitude of hers! That arrogance!

Facing her in the mirror, perhaps only three feet and a thin piece of glass away, the hottest looking woman that Jesse had seen in quite some time just stood there taking off her clothes . . .

Alex unclasped the last of her buttons. There was something about seeing her reflection, partially clothed, half dressed for a business meeting, half dressed for sex, that really aroused her.

She walked over to her suitcase, opened it and pulled out a small tape cassette player, plugging it in

by the nightstand. Her favorite song began to play. Slowly, she allowed herself to sway back and forth with the beat.

"The only one, the only one for me . . ." she sang softly as she turned off the bright overhead light leaving the room suggestively dimmed.

She danced back over to the mirror. As if performing for an audience, she moved quite erotically, slowly running her hands through the thick jungle of curls, seductively rotating her hips, permitting the blouse to slide down her shoulders and then on to the floor. She wore only the camisole, garter belt, stockings and heels.

She couldn't help but notice her dark red triangle of hair that was exposed as soon as her blouse had been removed, God, she loved her pussy! Just to look at it! First at a distance, then slowly spreading it apart, she examined every little crevice. That was the *very* thing that aroused her every time, what she looked forward to at the end of a busy, difficult day . . . pleasing herself in this way.

Jesse stood, glued to her spot, watching Ms. Tarree who was dancing most alluringly in front of the mirror. When she dropped that blouse to expose the magnificent patch of red hair pushing itself out from the confines of that remarkable garter belt, Jesse felt an intense pulsating in her own pussy.

If she could have any wish at all, it would be to see more of Ms. Tarree — those breasts that brushed back and forth beneath the shiny satin camisole . . . her nipples, erect from the constant grazing of the material across them. To see what was under that triangular curtain of red hair would be the hottest thing of all. Jesse liked nothing better than to be able to have a full view of a pussy in front of her, especially one that she had never seen before. She had spent some time looking through those magazines with the women spreading themselves open — plenty of time looking at those — but there was nothing like the real thing, especially on a hotshot woman like Ms. Tarree who was slowly lifting that lacy camisole right over her thick red mane.

And what a sight those breasts were! Not too small, not too large, they were perfect, as far as Jesse's taste went. They looked like peaches, a fine contrast to the dark red hair, with tips that appeared to have been dipped in pale pink paint. And then, as if the artist had used the finest of sable brushes, the nipples were tinted in a cherry red hue. The color was extraordinary, when one considered how light Ms. Tarree's skin was in comparison to the brightness of the nipples themselves.

Jesse could hardly believe what she was seeing: Ms. Tarree was sitting in front of the mirror, leaning back just a bit and placing each foot against the mirror, opening her legs, fully exposing her bushy nest of hair.

Jesse, as if truly believing she was all along invited to be a party to this show, sat on the floor directly in front of Ms. Tarree's secret sex nest. Oh God! she thought. Please let her open that treasure up for me. Oh please!

And, as if in response to Jesse's wish, Ms. Tarree slid her forefingers down into the curly hair and

160

pulled the large outer lips apart, exposing the hooded pink princess.

Jesse was beside herself in sexual heat. Ms. Tarree's pussy was the exact same cherry red color as her nipples — as if the tissue had been licked and sucked for quite awhile.

With her legs spread at a good forty-five degree angle, and those spiked high heels pushing against the mirror, Ms. Tarree's erect cherry was plainly in sight.

Ms. Tarree . . . oh really, who was she kidding at this point? It would never be "Ms. Tarree" again, not to Jesse anyway! It was Alex. After all, she was getting to know Alex quite well. Why keep the false pretense between them after such intimacy?

So there Alex was pushing up against the mirror, forcing her legs even further apart, beginning to work that almond-shaped skirt of tissue with her fingers.

With each small stroke, the large lips separated further apart, lifting the skin, exposing the glistening red clit. Flipping her finger, barely touching it really, she grazed it just enough for that hardened clitoris to poke its head out in hungry anticipation of each stroke.

The pussy itself was only inches away from the mirror. It was incredible how far Alex was able to spread her legs, to get so close to the mirror. Jesse — was it her imagination — could see the lightest film of steam on the glass from the heat of that opened, accordion-like pussy.

Jesse lay flat on the floor, trying to keep that cleaved, pleated pussy in sight, imagining what that marvelous, luscious little rosebud must taste like,

161

smell like. Barely a few inches away from the completely exposed, plump pink tissues, Jesse watched feverishly as Alex rubbed back and forth, faster and faster.

The sound of the bell dinging insistently at the front counter broke her from her frenzy. Quickly, Jesse closed the curtain and hurried out to the front desk.

"Oh good! We were worried that no one was here. Guess you didn't hear us at first."

"I'm so sorry, got caught up in some work in the back office and . . . you been here long?" Jesse said trying to appear normal, trying to hide how out of herself she felt at that very moment.

There were two women, one quite butch-looking and one rather femme. They were wrapped up in each other's arms . . . kissing and hanging all over each other.

"We'd like a room for the night. Got anything available at this hour?" the taller, more dominant-appearing woman said with a smile.

"Sure do . . ." Jesse reached in the drawer and pulled out the registration form, handing it to the woman. She couldn't concentrate; her mind was still on the mirror, inches away from Alex's hot red puckered pussy. Not one customer all night and then at the most crucial moment, in they walk, Jesse thought as the woman handed her back the form.

"Room number eight, around the side to the left. Need some help?" Jesse asked, praying that the women would do it all on their own. How difficult could it be to find room eight? She was busy, in the middle of something most important, surely that was obvious.

162

The femme was whispering something to her lover; her face had a slight flush to it, as if she was embarrassed about something.

Jesse was so aroused that her pussy was aching. Did she smell like sex? Is that why these women were whispering, looking at her so strangely?

"Yes," the butch woman said, smiling slyly. "We most certainly could use your help."

Damn, Jesse thought. That takes care of Alex.

"Okay, right this way," she replied, trying to keep the anger out of her voice. As if this woman really needed her help!

Jesse escorted the women into the room. She walked over to the floor lamp and turned it on.

"If you find that you need anything, just give me a holler." She turned to find the two women kissing quite intensely.

"As a matter of fact," the butch woman said in a husky voice as she closed the door behind her. "There is something that we need from you." The other woman was looking silently down at the floor. "I'm Nance, this is Lisa," the butch continued, looking directly across the room into Jesse's eyes. "Lisa tells me that she thinks you're rather attractive."

Jesse glanced at Lisa, a pretty woman, with long blonde hair surrounding her face like a halo of light.

"And she's quite picky about these sorts of things," Nance added. Her voice had a suggestive tone to it. "Are you really in that big of a hurry to get back to your office work?"

Jesse, surprised, was quiet. What did she want to hurry back to? A mirror that looked into a room where her Alex was probably in bed by this time. And here, like a gift from the gods, were two women who, if she was not mistaken, were coming on to her. She was already aroused from her ordeal with Alex . . . and *that* certainly wasn't going to go much further. Wouldn't it be nice to see what room eight had in store for her?

"Well," Jesse answered hesitantly, "I suppose what I was working on could wait a bit . . ."

"Good," Nance said coolly, taking Lisa by the hand and leading her toward the bathroom. "Why don't you slip into something more comfortable, honey, while me and — " she turned to Jesse with a questioning look on her face.

"Jesse."

"Yes. While me and Jesse get more acquainted."

Lisa obediently walked into the bathroom and closed the door.

Nance turned to Jesse and said matter-of-factly. "It's very simple what I'd like you to do. All I ask is that you follow along. If I ask you to do something that feels uncomfortable, there's no problem. Just shake your head. Sound okay with you?"

"Sure," Jesse replied, still hot from watching Alex. At this point, she was game for anything. It was going to be a most interesting night after all!

Suddenly the bathroom door opened and Lisa walked out with nothing on except for a thin cotton T-shirt. Without a word, without looking at Jesse directly, she walked over to the bed.

Lisa's perfectly raised, heart-shaped ass swayed flirtatiously as she moved toward the bed. She teased expertly, as if her ass had been created for one purpose only.

Jesse could feel her own pussy lubricate in anticipation of what she imagined would follow.

Lisa sat on the bed, slowly leaning back, pushing herself further on top of the bed.

Jesse was having trouble not staring directly at Lisa's down-covered pussy. The hair was so light in color that Jesse could already see the puckered flesh that protruded slightly from the lips.

"It's okay," Nance murmured, as if she could read Jesse's mind. "Go to her, have a closer look."

Lisa, waiting on the bed, smiled shyly. There was something about Jesse that was most appealing. She liked the stocky build, the short hair that had a roughness to it, the tight jeans that showed off her well-shaped legs and ass. Probably a body builder, Lisa thought.

She loved it when Nance would set these situations up for her. The sex was always so charged, and without exception it would vary; she could never be quite sure of how Nance would carry it off. Nance, her lover of three years, took care of her every need, her every wish.

Jesse approached the bed with a fiery look in her eye, as though she had been sitting around all evening, waiting for this sort of thing to happen.

Nance said in a low voice, "I want you to take a close look at Lisa's pussy, it's really quite extraordinary — for such a petite woman! Come, let me show you."

She guided Jesse to the bed. Lisa was lying back, her legs propped on the edge of the bed, each knee having fallen aside, allowing enough room for Jesse in between them.

Jesse, looking down at Lisa's pussy, could scarcely believe the set of circumstances she had found herself in — first the intoxicating experience with hot Alex, and now this most intriguing arena of sex.

Nance leaned over from Jesse's right side and gently opened the thick blonde covered lips.

"There," she said seductively. "Isn't that the prettiest pussy you've ever seen?"

Jesse watched, hypnotized, as Nance spread even further the large outer lips.

"What I'd like, what I'd really like to see," Nance suggested, "is your finger just lightly touching along the sides of Lisa's clitoris. How does that sound to you, Lisa?"

"Oh, Nance, you know everything I like, don't you?" Lisa sighed.

"Of course I do . . . and I know that Jesse here would like nothing more than to touch you that way. Right, Jesse? Go ahead, lick your finger, that's good, and run it . . . no don't touch the clit yet! Yes that's right, just run your finger up and down the space between — "

Jesse, following Nance's instruction, let her finger lightly travel in that smooth crevice between the fleshy tissue and the lip. It took a tremendous amount of self-control to keep her finger from flicking across that large red flange of tissue. She continued to glide her finger up and down ever so slightly, quite aware that she was cheating, just the slightest bit. She was applying just the smallest amount of pressure, causing her finger to barely lean on that off-limits enticing clitoral flesh.

"Now," Nance said breathlessly, "I want you to

166

see how firm, how erect Lisa is under that little hump of flesh."

It was quite deceiving really, she appeared so spongy, but, as Jesse permitted her finger the luxury of nudging against the cleft of deep pink tissue, the entire flap was even thicker than she had anticipated. She had slept with her share of women, but had never encountered a pussy that was so open, so large and protruding! It was exquisite.

No longer having to accidentally touch that knot of tissue, she had full permission to rub her greedy finger back and forth over that stub of flesh. How hard it was!

Lisa was moaning in pleasure as Jesse continued to slide her finger across her slick shaft. She arched, trying to position herself this way and that, to follow Jesse's wandering fingertip.

"Hold yourself apart, Lisa, now I want to watch Jesse lick that sweet sugar pussy of yours." Nance continued to monitor the steamy sex scene under her direction. "Jesse, force the tip of your tongue into a point like this. Can you point your tongue like this?" she said, pushing her own tongue out of her mouth. "Oh, yes, Jesse, that's perfect. Run it up and down the side of her clit like you did at first with your finger. But don't touch it yet . . . wait till you see how hard this gets her. Right, Lisa?"

Lisa was barely able to respond, she was so totally immersed in sexual tension. She wanted more. Eyes closed, she listened to her lover instructing that hot stranger to rub her, to tongue her.

"Now, lightly, this is important, I want you to let your tongue lap. Pretend you're a little kitty and we

167

coated Lisa's pussy with honey . . . Lap like that . . ."

Jesse, placing her tongue on that mound of flesh, was overwhelmed. An exotic fragrance emanated from Lisa's incredible pussy. Jesse gently prodded that hard, bulbous clit as though trying to coax it to a new place on her pussy.

"Here," Nance whispered, "put your tongue in this."

She handed Jesse a small latex cuff to slide her tongue into. It was smooth on the inside where her tongue slid in, but delicately roughened on the outside . . . almost the same texture as a kitten's tongue.

"Go ahead, Jesse, lap her off with that."

She carefully lapped the entire length of Lisa's clitoris. Was she imagining the slight scraping sound she heard as she licked Lisa's pussy with the small sandpaper jacket on her tongue?

Lisa's body was rigid in pleasure, arched up and frozen as Jesse continued to suck every possible bit of sweetness of that honey-dipped pussy.

Jesse, her face saturated with Lisa's sex oil, was engrossed in the constant scraping with her tongue. There was just the slightest resistance as the roughened cuff slid over the delicate tissues, causing her own pussy to ache with desire. Lifting Lisa's ass, cupping her hands around the firm round cheeks, Jesse held her at the perfect angle. Lisa opened even further with each stroke from Jesse's tongue.

Jesse felt Nance moving behind her. She unsnapped Jesse's jeans, tugging them down below her knees, and finally caressing her full ass.

"And what about you?" Nance was murmuring. "What's your pussy wanting just about now?" With great ease, she was able to slip her fingers under Jesse's drenched panties, up in between the generous folds of skin.

Jesse worked Lisa's pussy with the cat-tongue sheath, let a small cry escape from her lips as Nance began to thump Jesse's shaft quite vigorously. Nance centered on the very spot that had throbbed so desperately moments before.

Both Jesse and Lisa entered into orgasm at the same time. Lisa yelped in ecstasy and Jesse forced her face deeper into Lisa's dampness, nearly smothering in pleasure as she continued to feel Nance's finger whipping her pounding clitoris over and over in rhythm with Jesse's lapping.

Lisa collapsed down onto the bed, Jesse fell directly on top of her, and Nance stretched out alongside both of them.

"Aren't you glad you decided to stay?" Nance said with a small laugh.

"The best decision I've made in a long time." Jesse sighed, lazily glancing at her watch. "Oh my God!" she stammered. "I can't believe how long I've been here! I'm the only one on duty. I've got to get back to the front counter before I get into deep shit!" She groaned, pulling up her pants quickly.

"Well, we sure had a nice time, didn't we Lisa?"

"Yes, most definitely!" Lisa said as she sat up, running her hands through her tangled hair. "Come back later if you can." She smiled seductively.

"That I will!" Jesse said, leaning over and giving her a kiss on the lips, then doing the same to Nance.

169

Quickly she snapped her pants closed and hurried back to the lobby.

"Oh, you are open!" the woman said, turning to face Jesse as she rushed into the lobby. "I was beginning to think the ship had been abandoned!"

"So sorry!" Jesse said, trying to catch her breath. What a night! What a night! What a night! she thought. "Have you been waiting long?"

"No, not that long really . . . your phone rang but I didn't think I should answer it."

"Got stuck giving a hand to some of the lodgers . . . "You looking for a room?"

"Oh, no, I'm staying with friends on the east side . . . they told me about this resort and I was wondering if I could use some space here to hold a pleasure party for your patrons."

"A pleasure party?" Jesse asked, intrigued by the charming woman. "What's a pleasure party?"

"Could we talk back there?" the woman said, gesturing toward the back office.

"I suppose we could step into the office," Jesse replied, knowing that she was breaking yet another rule.

"I'm Susan," the woman said, extending a hand.

"I'm Jesse." Jesse shook Susan's hand and then ushered her into the small back office. The drape was still slightly askew from where Jesse had been watching Alex earlier that evening.

Susan walked over to the coffee table, placing her two small suitcases on top, and said matter-of-factly, "I like to go to the most popular women's resorts during the summer and hold these pleasure parties for the guests. It always turns out to be a hit — everybody has a good time — and I have a chance to do some business."

"So what exactly is a pleasure party?" Jesse asked again as Susan opened one of the cases.

"Well, for example, I sell lingerie . . . like this or this . . ." Susan held up a black negligee and a red garter belt.

"That kind of stuff doesn't really look so hot on me." Jesse's voice had a slight sarcastic tone.

"Perhaps not for you . . . but maybe on your lover? Look at what a difference an article of clothing can make . . . Turn around for just a minute and I'll show you what I mean."

Jesse, not quite sure what to expect next after the evening's events, turned her back on Susan.

"Okay! You can turn around now!" Susan exclaimed.

Jesse turned back to Susan to see her standing there wearing nothing but a very revealing, black lace nightgown.

"As I said," Susan continued softly, "perhaps not for you . . ."

Jesse stood, stunned, staring at Susan. She was incredibly appealing, her full breasts barely covered by the lacy silk material.

"And I'm sure what I have in the other suitcase will interest you a bit more." Susan unsnapped the other case.

"You see, I have something for everyone," she murmured as she tilted the suitcase for Jesse to peek in at the contents.

The suitcase was filled with a variety of sex toys,

171

some of which Jesse had never seen before . . . including a small package of the tongue cuffs that she had used on Lisa not long before.

"And look! Look at this," Susan said enticingly as she lifted out a two-headed vibrator. "Have you ever seen anything so extraordinary?"

"To tell you the truth, I've never been one to get into those types of things."

"That's the whole fun of a pleasure party. There's things in here that most women haven't ever tried before . . . and what could be more fun than trying something new? Like this vibrator, for instance," she said eagerly as she hunted for an electrical outlet. "Here, now take a look at how this thing works."

Susan plugged in the vibrator and sat down on a nearby stool. She lifted her nightie and spread her legs far apart, exposing her small fur-lined pussy.

"It's very deceiving the way this thing works . . . perhaps you should come a little closer."

Although she had been completely satisfied by Lisa and Nance, when Jesse saw Susan's legs open wide and her lips begin to spread apart, she was once again consumed with desire. This was the very thing that Jesse felt to be irresistible — that first peek at a woman's secret place.

"So easy to sell really," Susan was saying, inserting the narrower tip into her slippery vagina and resting the other, more bulblike vibrator head on her tucked-in clitoris. She quickly clicked on the button causing the room to fill with a low humming sound.

Jesse, almost in a trance, moved closer, then even

closer. No longer trying to keep up pretenses, she fell to her knees directly in front of Susan's pussy.

"That's right," Susan moaned. "Touch the other side of my clit . . . you'll see what a nice steady beat this has."

Jesse placed her finger on the glossy flap of tissue and felt it vibrating rapidly.

"And notice, if you will," Susan whispered, "how I'm able to slowly move the other head in and out of myself as I stimulate my clitoris at the same time! Quite revolutionary I'd say!"

"Yes," Jesse said, breathless herself, wanting only to crush her face against Susan's pussy with its most intoxicating fragrance. That flabby tuft of tissue vibrated at such an entrancing speed . . .

Suddenly, without time to think things through, Jesse pulled the vibrator to the side and forced her hungry tongue between the lips to the very center of that perfumed opening. Lapping wildly, she grabbed Susan's ass to try to hold her on the stool while she sucked continuously — licking, drinking in the sweetness. Drunk from the taste, she urgently thrust her tongue into the yielding candied slit, desperately taking the entire shaft into her mouth and burying her face deeper and deeper into the satiny folds of skin.

Susan, leaning against the wall in an attempt to balance herself, grabbed the vibrator from Jesse's hand and placed it back on her swollen jewel.

"Keep sucking! Keep sucking while I use this!" Susan cried. She slid the vibrator down to where Jesse's tongue was ravenously devouring her.

Jesse continued to lick as best she could. It felt as if her nose and tongue were vibrating along with the massager's head as they greedily fought to share Susan's pussy. Faster and faster, both the machine and Jesse's tongue pulsated.

Suddenly, Susan let out a loud moan, as she grabbed Jesse's hair. Bucking wildly in deep pleasure, her entire body shuddered as she entered into orgasm, moaning, "Yes, baby! Oh yes baby!"

Jesse, unable to contain herself any longer, flung the vibrator onto the floor.

This is for me now, all for me, she thought as she continued to suck madly on Susan's quivering pussy. Barely able to breathe, she sank her entire face into the sopping wet folds of skin. She was hardly conscious of anything else but the delicious tangy taste, the musky inviting scent. This was it, heaven, as far as Jesse was concerned . . . and within seconds she felt herself igniting into her own orgasm.

Jesse lunged deeper between Susan's legs, holding on tightly and then letting go, falling backwards onto the floor with a sigh.

"You see," Susan said with a smile, "the product sells itself!"

Jesse let out a laugh, only to be interrupted by the sound of the bell being hit demandingly at the front counter.

"Oh God!" she said nervously as she pulled herself up from the floor and dried her face, which was absolutely soaked from sex, on her sleeve. "Do you think anyone heard us?"

Susan shrugged. Jesse walked out to the front desk.

"Shit!" Jesse said under her breath. Alex Tarree was at the counter tapping her fingers angrily.

"Well, it's about time. I tried to phone and obviously you were *too* busy to take any calls from your clients. I suppose your manager doesn't really have a clue as to what kind of help she has here, does she!"

"What's the matter, does Alex have herself a little problem that she can't take care of herself? Seems to me you're pretty good at tending to your own needs!" Jesse said sarcastically. She'd had it with the bitch. Who the hell did she think she was? When it came right down to it, Alex Tarree was no better than anyone else.

As if flabbergasted that someone could have the nerve to speak to her in such a way, Alex just stood there with a shocked expression on her face.

"That's right," Jesse continued, getting somewhat carried away with her new-found attitude. "I don't have to take shit from you, and I don't give a damn *who* you tell! Now what is it you need?"

"Ice. As soon as possible," Alex said coldly.

"There's an ice machine right by room eight. Help yourself!"

Alex walked briskly out of the lobby, slamming the screen door behind her.

Susan, hearing the door slam, quickly closed the drape she had pulled aside, still somewhat fascinated by the two-way glass she had discovered.

"Jesse? Are you okay?" Susan asked, peeking her head around the corner.

"Yeah," Jesse replied, still caught off guard by her less-than-professional behavior with Alex. "I just

kind of lost it with that woman . . . I'll be okay."
She met Susan in the office doorway and gave her a
kiss.

"Who was that anyway?" Susan asked, looking
over Jesse's shoulder toward the screen door as she
finished buttoning her blouse.

"She comes in here today like she's somebody
special — treating me like I'm some sort of nobody.
Really got to me . . . but I don't just take that kind
of crap, no way! I've got my own way of making
things even." Jesse glanced at the covered two-way
mirror with a highly self-satisfied expression on her
face.

Yeah, I'll bet! Susan thought, checking her watch.
"Oh my! Look at the time. I've really got to get
going," she said, quickly giving Jesse another light
kiss on the cheek and then looking around the room
to make sure she had retrieved all of her belongings.
"So, what do you think about letting me do a party
here?"

"It's fine with me, but there aren't too many
women here . . . not until mid-June."

"That's fine. I'm going to be in town a few
weeks, perhaps we could see each other again? I've
left you a card with the number where I'm staying.
Also there's a little something for you in the bag."

Jesse looked over to the table, at a brown paper
bag.

"Hope to hear from you soon," Susan said with a
wink. She turned and left.

Jesse walked over to the bag. She pulled out a
medium-sized one-headed vibrator with a small note
attached to it . . . *Go ahead try me.*

Jesse let a smile escape her lips. She hadn't had

this much sex in a long time — it had been a most unbelievable night. She put the vibrator down and started back into the lobby, to relax, to finish that book of stories Bev had brought her, but suddenly she heard just the slightest nagging from inside her mind. *Go ahead, try it . . . you saw how good Susan came. Have you ever seen anyone come that good before? Nooooooo. Go ahead. Try it.*

Jesse walked back to the table and took the vibrator out of the bag again. It was getting late . . . and no one would be coming around any more tonight. What did she have to lose?

She plugged it in near the draped two-way mirror, pulled her snug jeans down and let the padded vibrator head rest on her thick, dark mound of hair. She clicked the small machine on and it began to vibrate immediately. Jesse felt an intense tingling shoot through her pussy. "Holy shit!" she said aloud. She had never felt anything like *that* sensation before.

The vibrator tapped lightly against her pussy and that same feeling rushed through her once again. Now, all she could really think of was getting those jeans off completely, lying on the floor with her legs spread as far as possible, and holding that incredibly pulsating tip on her aroused clitoris.

Within seconds, she was on the floor allowing the padded head to gently beat down on her entire pussy. She thought about the day's events: Susan on the stool with her legs spread, that intoxicating pussy entrancing Jesse with its fragrance; Lisa leaning back on the bed as Nance instructed Jesse how to lap her like a kitten — how very nasty! And Alex, that bitch of a hot woman, spread in front of her on the floor,

177

watching her own pussy in the mirror, believing she was all alone. To think Jesse was only inches away from that thick beet-red cunt!

Desperately, Jesse pulled the drape aside, wanting only to push her legs up against the glass as Alex had, remembering how that wide-open gaping pussy steamed the mirror! Quickly, she positioned herself. She looked up into the glass, imagining her side was also mirrored . . .

But Jesse's fantasy was momentarily put aside when she looked up into the glass and saw Alex wrapped in a robe, sitting at a table in her room laughing with Susan. They were sipping, was it champagne? Susan had her case open and was showing Alex the double-headed vibrator. They were talking vivaciously, or so it appeared. Her eyes were searching the room. Oh yes, Jesse recognized that "where's the outlet" look.

"Come on," Jesse whispered, placing her own vibrator back onto her yearning pussy. "It's by the mirror . . . find the outlet by the mirror."

Susan was standing, still talking away, and then just as Jesse had hoped, she walked over to the mirror and plugged it in. "That's a girl," Jesse murmured. "Bring her over to the mirror. Let me see that bitch use it on her pussy, right here, right in front of me."

As if the two women could hear Jesse's pleas, they moved over to the mirror, with Alex spread-eagled on the floor, feet propped up on the glass, and Susan kneeling at her side.

"That's right." Jesse was moaning, still lightly touching the vibrator to her own swollen clitoris.

"Spread her apart, let me see it again . . . Oh, that's just what I want."

Jesse swore they could hear her through that thin glass. Alex spread her full lips apart as Susan placed the two-headed vibrator between her legs. Jesse could see Alex's body jerk just a bit when the narrower tip was inserted into the little lips that surrounded the opening of Alex's tight slit. At the same time, Susan let the other head gently brush against Alex's fat, hardened shaft.

Jesse could not believe how hot she felt — her own vibrator increasing in intensity as she allowed the head to lie on her throbbing clit with a bit more pressure. And there was Alex, across from her, doing the same thing. Susan had gotten up and was moving over to the table. Why was she stopping? Please not now! Jesse begged. Please!

Susan reached into the ice bucket and returned to Alex with a sexy grin on her face. She was saying something to Alex, running her hands through Alex's tangled hair, whispering in Alex's ear, or so it seemed. She did see Alex raise up on her elbows just a bit, as if she wanted to get a better look in the mirror . . .

And now, Susan was taking — could it be? She was taking an ice cube and running it up the inside of Alex's firm, rounded thigh, slowly gliding it up one side, across the red mound and down the other thigh.

"Go ahead, go ahead!" Jesse panted. "Put it on that Ice Princess's cherry red pussy!"

Again, Susan slid the ice cube across the soft nest of hair, getting closer, even closer to that mesmerizing pink flower.

179

Teasingly, Susan slightly skidded it onto the lips, circling it deep enough so that the cube began to burrow its way into the blooming crimson bud.

Alex arched in pleasure as the droplets of ice water haphazardly dripped onto her torrid pussy. Jesse sat up, moving in closer to the mirror in order to examine in detail each place Susan tapped with that cool cube. She wanted to see every little crevice, every little color change, every reaction to the ice that first stunned, then aroused.

She was not disappointed. Alex's tissues were responding quickly to the freezing. The cleft of clitoral tissue swelled and when Susan pulled back the lip of the miniature hood the little bead was a deep magenta.

Once again, Jesse turned on her vibrator and placed it on her aching clit. Once more the intense pulsating began. She kept staring as though trying to memorize every inch of Alex's pussy. Closing her eyes, she compared Alex's pussy to Susan's, then to Lisa's, and then to a December, 1987 centerfold that she had never, ever forgotten! Each pussy was close up, spread apart, smelling, tasting, feeling — the images swirled. Jesse exploded into the most incredible orgasm she had ever had.

She fell back onto the floor with a moan. How long she stayed like that she wasn't really sure, but when she sat up both Susan and Alex were gone.

Jesse pulled herself up, ran her hands through her hair and let out a small whistle. "Pretty hot!" she said, shaking her head. She dropped the vibrator into the brown bag. To think she'd gotten one over on Alex — renting room four to her, taking advantage of the situation for her own pleasure, feeling like she had gotten the best of that bitch by seeing her spread open like that . . . Jesse let out a satisfied laugh. "What you don't know won't hurt you, Ms. Tarree!"

Jesse, feeling smug, pulled her pants back on and went back to the lobby, sat in the chair, and reached for her book.

The thinnest sheet of expensive note paper drifted out of the book and floated gracefully to the floor. Jesse leaned over and picked it up.

"Dear Jesse . . ."

How very fine the penmanship! How painstakingly the writer must have concentrated! Every word slanted just so, the curve of each letter perfectly executed, rising and confidently sloping into the next. There was a certain haughtiness, a brazenness really, if one felt the need to interpret *this* particular handwriting in such a personal way.

". . . The absolute *hottest* part of all was knowing that you were watching. Alex."

Jesse felt her body tighten with a sudden outrage. Infuriated, she wadded the note into a ball and tossed it into the trash. She opened the book, wanting only to escape into the fantasy world of fiction where things were much, much easier to deal with.

"Hey, Jesse . . . Lady! C'mon wake up!" Bev was shaking Jesse from a deep sleep. Her legs were still propped up and her head leaned over the side of the chair; she was clutching tightly the book Bev had lent her earlier that evening. "C'mon, wake up, your shift is over in five minutes." She glanced over to the empty guest register and whispered into Jesse's ear, "Slow night, huh?"

Startled, Jesse opened her eyes, accidentally dropping the book as she shifted in the chair.

Bev quickly bent down and retrieved the book and nonchalantly began flipping through the pages.

"That's one hot book!" Jesse said, more awake, sitting up in the chair, stretching fully.

"So much for 'I don't read that summer vacation romance shit,' " Bev said with a cocksure grin.

"Yeah," Jesse said with a sigh of satisfaction as she glanced at the title. "PLEASURES."

A few of the publications of
THE NAIAD PRESS, INC.
P.O. Box 10543 ● Tallahassee, Florida 32302
Phone (904) 539-5965
Mail orders welcome. Please include 15% postage.

PLEASURES by Robbi Sommers. 204 pp. Unprecedented
eroticism. ISBN 0-941483-49-5 $8.95

EDGEWISE by Camarin Grae. 372 pp. Spellbinding
adventure. ISBN 0-941483-19-3   9.95

FATAL REUNION by Claire McNab. 216 pp. 2nd Det. Inspec.
Carol Ashton mystery. ISBN 0-941483-40-1   8.95

KEEP TO ME STRANGER by Sarah Aldridge. 372 pp. Romance
set in a department store dynasty. ISBN 0-941483-38-X   9.95

HEARTSCAPE by Sue Gambill. 204 pp. American lesbian in
Portugal. ISBN 0-941483-33-9   8.95

IN THE BLOOD by Lauren Wright Douglas. 252 pp. Lesbian
science fiction adventure fantasy ISBN 0-941483-22-3   8.95

THE BEE'S KISS by Shirley Verel. 216 pp. Delicate, delicious
romance. ISBN 0-941483-36-3   8.95

RAGING MOTHER MOUNTAIN by Pat Emmerson. 264 pp.
Furosa Firechild's adventures in Wonderland. ISBN 0-941483-35-5   8.95

IN EVERY PORT by Karin Kallmaker. 228 pp. Jessica's sexy,
adventuresome travels. ISBN 0-941483-37-7   8.95

OF LOVE AND GLORY by Evelyn Kennedy. 192 pp. Exciting
WWII romance. ISBN 0-941483-32-0   8.95

CLICKING STONES by Nancy Tyler Glenn. 288 pp. Love
transcending time. ISBN 0-941483-31-2   8.95

SURVIVING SISTERS by Gail Pass. 252 pp. Powerful love
story. ISBN 0-941483-16-9   8.95

SOUTH OF THE LINE by Catherine Ennis. 216 pp. Civil War
adventure. ISBN 0-941483-29-0   8.95

WOMAN PLUS WOMAN by Dolores Klaich. 300 pp. Supurb
Lesbian overview. ISBN 0-941483-28-2   9.95

SLOW DANCING AT MISS POLLY'S by Sheila Ortiz Taylor.
96 pp. Lesbian Poetry ISBN 0-941483-30-4   7.95

DOUBLE DAUGHTER by Vicki P. McConnell. 216 pp. A Nyla
Wade Mystery, third in the series. ISBN 0-941483-26-6   8.95

HEAVY GILT by Delores Klaich. 192 pp. Lesbian detective/
disappearing homophobes/upper class gay society.

                                      ISBN 0-941483-25-8   8.95

THE FINER GRAIN by Denise Ohio. 216 pp. Brilliant young college lesbian novel. ISBN 0-941483-11-8   8.95

THE AMAZON TRAIL by Lee Lynch. 216 pp. Life, travel & lore of famous lesbian author. ISBN 0-941483-27-4   8.95

HIGH CONTRAST by Jessie Lattimore. 264 pp. Women of the Crystal Palace. ISBN 0-941483-17-7   8.95

OCTOBER OBSESSION by Meredith More. Josie's rich, secret Lesbian life. ISBN 0-941483-18-5   8.95

LESBIAN CROSSROADS by Ruth Baetz. 276 pp. Contemporary Lesbian lives. ISBN 0-941483-21-5   9.95

BEFORE STONEWALL: THE MAKING OF A GAY AND LESBIAN COMMUNITY by Andrea Weiss & Greta Schiller. 96 pp., 25 illus. ISBN 0-941483-20-7   7.95

WE WALK THE BACK OF THE TIGER by Patricia A. Murphy. 192 pp. Romantic Lesbian novel/beginning women's movement. ISBN 0-941483-13-4   8.95

SUNDAY'S CHILD by Joyce Bright. 216 pp. Lesbian athletics, at last the novel about sports. ISBN 0-941483-12-6   8.95

OSTEN'S BAY by Zenobia N. Vole. 204 pp. Sizzling adventure romance set on Bonaire. ISBN 0-941483-15-0   8.95

LESSONS IN MURDER by Claire McNab. 216 pp. 1st Det. Inspec. Carol Ashton mystery — erotic tension!. ISBN 0-941483-14-2   8.95

YELLOWTHROAT by Penny Hayes. 240 pp. Margarita, bandit, kidnaps Julia. ISBN 0-941483-10-X   8.95

SAPPHISTRY: THE BOOK OF LESBIAN SEXUALITY by Pat Califia. 3d edition, revised. 208 pp. ISBN 0-941483-24-X   8.95

CHERISHED LOVE by Evelyn Kennedy. 192 pp. Erotic Lesbian love story. ISBN 0-941483-08-8   8.95

LAST SEPTEMBER by Helen R. Hull. 208 pp. Six stories & a glorious novella. ISBN 0-941483-09-6   8.95

THE SECRET IN THE BIRD by Camarin Grae. 312 pp. Striking, psychological suspense novel. ISBN 0-941483-05-3   8.95

TO THE LIGHTNING by Catherine Ennis. 208 pp. Romantic Lesbian 'Robinson Crusoe' adventure. ISBN 0-941483-06-1   8.95

THE OTHER SIDE OF VENUS by Shirley Verel. 224 pp. Luminous, romantic love story. ISBN 0-941483-07-X   8.95

DREAMS AND SWORDS by Katherine V. Forrest. 192 pp. Romantic, erotic, imaginative stories. ISBN 0-941483-03-7   8.95

MEMORY BOARD by Jane Rule. 336 pp. Memorable novel about an aging Lesbian couple ISBN 0-941483-02-9   8.95

THE ALWAYS ANONYMOUS BEAST by Lauren Wright
Douglas. 224 pp. A Caitlin Reese mystery. First in a series.
ISBN 0-941483-04-5   8.95

SEARCHING FOR SPRING by Patricia A. Murphy. 224 pp.
Novel about the recovery of love.   ISBN 0-941483-00-2   8.95

DUSTY'S QUEEN OF HEARTS DINER by Lee Lynch. 240 pp.
Romantic blue-collar novel.   ISBN 0-941483-01-0   8.95

PARENTS MATTER by Ann Muller. 240 pp. Parents'
relationships with Lesbian daughters and gay sons.
ISBN 0-930044-91-6   9.95

THE PEARLS by Shelley Smith. 176 pp. Passion and fun in
the Caribbean sun.   ISBN 0-930044-93-2   7.95

MAGDALENA by Sarah Aldridge. 352 pp. Epic Lesbian novel
set on three continents.   ISBN 0-930044-99-1   8.95

THE BLACK AND WHITE OF IT by Ann Allen Shockley.
144 pp. Short stories.   ISBN 0-930044-96-7   7.95

SAY JESUS AND COME TO ME by Ann Allen Shockley. 288
pp. Contemporary romance.   ISBN 0-930044-98-3   8.95

LOVING HER by Ann Allen Shockley. 192 pp. Romantic love
story.   ISBN 0-930044-97-5   7.95

MURDER AT THE NIGHTWOOD BAR by Katherine V.
Forrest. 240 pp. A Kate Delafield mystery. Second in a series.
ISBN 0-930044-92-4   8.95

ZOE'S BOOK by Gail Pass. 224 pp. Passionate, obsessive love
story.   ISBN 0-930044-95-9   7.95

WINGED DANCER by Camarin Grae. 228 pp. Erotic Lesbian
adventure story.   ISBN 0-930044-88-6   8.95

PAZ by Camarin Grae. 336 pp. Romantic Lesbian adventurer
with the power to change the world.   ISBN 0-930044-89-4   8.95

SOUL SNATCHER by Camarin Grae. 224 pp. A puzzle, an
adventure, a mystery — Lesbian romance.   ISBN 0-930044-90-8   8.95

THE LOVE OF GOOD WOMEN by Isabel Miller. 224 pp.
Long-awaited new novel by the author of the beloved *Patience
and Sarah.*   ISBN 0-930044-81-9   8.95

THE HOUSE AT PELHAM FALLS by Brenda Weathers. 240
pp. Suspenseful Lesbian ghost story.   ISBN 0-930044-79-7   7.95

HOME IN YOUR HANDS by Lee Lynch. 240 pp. More stories
from the author of *Old Dyke Tales.*   ISBN 0-930044-80-0   7.95

EACH HAND A MAP by Anita Skeen. 112 pp. Real-life poems
that touch us all.   ISBN 0-930044-82-7   6.95

SURPLUS by Sylvia Stevenson. 342 pp. A classic early Lesbian
novel.   ISBN 0-930044-78-9   7.95

THE MARQUISE AND THE NOVICE by Victoria Ramstetter.
108 pp. A Lesbian Gothic novel.   ISBN 0-930044-16-9   6.95

OUTLANDER by Jane Rule. 207 pp. Short stories and essays
by one of our finest writers.   ISBN 0-930044-17-7   8.95

ALL TRUE LOVERS by Sarah Aldridge. 292 pp. Romantic
novel set in the 1930s and 1940s.   ISBN 0-930044-10-X   7.95

A WOMAN APPEARED TO ME by Renee Vivien. 65 pp. A
classic; translated by Jeannette H. Foster.   ISBN 0-930044-06-1   5.00

CYTHEREA'S BREATH by Sarah Aldridge. 240 pp. Romantic
novel about women's entrance into medicine.
                                           ISBN 0-930044-02-9   6.95

TOTTIE by Sarah Aldridge. 181 pp. Lesbian romance in the
turmoil of the sixties.   ISBN 0-930044-01-0   6.95

THE LATECOMER by Sarah Aldridge. 107 pp. A delicate love
story.   ISBN 0-930044-00-2   6.95

ODD GIRL OUT by Ann Bannon.   ISBN 0-930044-83-5   5.95

I AM A WOMAN by Ann Bannon.   ISBN 0-930044-84-3   5.95

WOMEN IN THE SHADOWS by Ann Bannon.
                                           ISBN 0-930044-85-1   5.95

JOURNEY TO A WOMAN by Ann Bannon.
                                           ISBN 0-930044-86-X   5.95

BEEBO BRINKER by Ann Bannon.   ISBN 0-930044-87-8   5.95
          Legendary novels written in the fifties and sixties,
              set in the gay mecca of Greenwich Village.

VOLUTE BOOKS

JOURNEY TO FULFILLMENT   Early classics by Valerie   3.95

A WORLD WITHOUT MEN   Taylor: The Erika Frohmann   3.95

RETURN TO LESBOS   series.   3.95

These are just a few of the many Naiad Press titles — we are the oldest and
largest lesbian/feminist publishing company in the world. Please request a
complete catalog. We offer personal service; we encourage and welcome
direct mail orders from individuals who have limited access to bookstores
carrying our publications.